For Joanne

Hope - you REVE.

luv The Immor...

THE IMMORTALS

THE IMMORTALS

BY

ALAN J. GOULD

www.bookstandpublishing.com

Published by
Bookstand Publishing
Morgan Hill, CA 95037
4308_5

ISBN 978-1-63498-176-7

Printed in the United States of America

DEDICATION

I'm deeply grateful to two wonderful people for whatever success I might achieve with this endeavor. First, to my beautiful wife, Marcy, without whose patience and caring it would not have happened. And to my friend and mentor, Sue Clark, whose encouragement and persistence made my efforts a reality.

ACKNOWLEDGEMENT

Dr. Abby Person, my lovely, talented niece, who provided the technical details on the genetic process. Bev Lauderdale, Elaine Starkman, Liz Rosner, and Sue Clark, my mentors, critics, absolutists all, without whose support and encouragement I never would have, could have attempted this project. Thank you.

CHAPTER ONE

David didn't pick up the telephone at first. He wasn't inclined to premonitions or such. Quite the contrary. However, he sat in the chair by the telephone table and picked up the receiver on the third ring.

"David, this is Tom."

He recognized the voice of his brother-in-law, even though he hadn't spoken to him for six months.

"There is no way I can say this easily. Are you sitting down?"

David felt the recurring pain in his left knee and reached for it with his free hand. "What happened to Lee?" he said.

"She died this morning. I'm…" Tom's voice broke.

David could hear deep breaths but didn't respond at once. The receiver slipped from his ear.

Lee's dead.

The words repeated in David's mind until the reality registered. "Where are you calling from?" he said.

"Vienna. Vienna, Virginia. I don't know what to say. I..."

"How did she die?" David interrupted. "What happened? An accident?"

The line was silent for a moment.

"It wasn't an accident. I can't discuss it over the phone. Will you come?"

Will I come? How to begin? Where to start? In the space of seconds, routine is interrupted by the intrusion of death. "I'll try to catch the ten o'clock United red-eye from SFO. That should get me into Dulles about six. Check the arrival time. I'll let you know if I can't make that flight."

"I'll be there, David." Tom paused, "Yes, I'll be there."

David returned the phone to the cradle. The pain in his left knee was on the anterior side, radiating into the calf. He extended the leg several times to stretch the muscles and then sat back in the chair. He shut his eyes and tried to picture his sister. They ran together during those golden years. How long ago could that have been? Was it only four or five years?

Without effort they'd run the trails along the East Bay and through the hills. Running with the fog swirling in the wind. He could see her with her hair tied by a kerchief into a ponytail trailing behind her — running on Christmas morning, seeing people through their windows, around the trees, in the evening as the sun set low in the west their shadows keeping pace, fast through the woods to finish before dark. They were immortal, they told each other, laughing. As long as they could run, they'd live forever. Now she was gone.

Gone in a one-minute phone conversation in which neither man could find anything meaningful to say to the other.

The plane arced in its descent to Dulles. David enjoyed traveling to Washington, especially in the fall when the leaves began to change and the wind from the west eased the summer heat. This trip was different, of course, and had been a struggle for him to pack. He didn't know how long he'd be staying. There'd be a funeral so he'd need a dark suit. He packed a small suitcase that would fit under the seat and also a garment bag for his suit, a light jacket, and extra slacks. If plans changed, he'd just buy what was needed. When the cabin lights dimmed, he tilted his seat back, rested his head, and stared at the darkness through the window.

CHAPTER TWO

David was jealous of him. He knew that. He and Lee were dependent on each other. No parents. He couldn't warm up to Tom. For Lee's sake he tried. Tom worked for the government or something, and everything was such a damn secret. Big deal. Didn't hear for months, not a call, not even a postcard. David just accepted it. And now this.

Their father died when David was eight years old. He recalled his mother standing between Lee and him, clutching their hands when the coffin was lowered. As they turned from the grave, she patted him on the head.

"You're the man of the family, now."

They lived in a three-bedroom house in Moraga, an upscale rural community, just east of the hills separating Oakland and Berkeley from the suburbs.

Their mother worked as a bookkeeper for a publishing company in San Francisco, although money wasn't a major consideration as their father had provided for his family. After Lee graduated from high school, she entered the University of California, Berkeley, majoring in English and living in a dorm on campus. After graduation, Lee obtained a position in a Berkeley bookstore and moved into her own apartment.

Upon graduation, and passing the bar, David moved into his own quarters in Oakland near the law firm where he began his internship. Lee and David met on Sundays for the required dinner with their mother. However, other than that, and the usual holidays, they weren't in regular contact, each busy establishing their careers and professional relationships. This changed when their mother died.

They sat in their mother's living room in Moraga trying to decide what to do with each of her items. How could they divide those things, separate the music box from the candlesticks, dishes from silverware, all the photographs documenting a shared lifetime?

"I've joined a running club," Lee announced over dinner one evening. "Some of my friends at the shop belong and they invited me, so I splurged for a pair of shoes, and I had fun. We jogged around the marina after work. I couldn't go far, out of shape I guess, but I'm committed. Want to give it a try?"

Running became their shared passion. Every evening, after work, they would run the hills, the Concord Canal Trail, the La Fayette/Moraga trail. They challenged each other on ten-kilometer races around Lake Merritt in Oakland and finally marathons. Her first was the San Francisco Marathon across the Golden Gate Bridge and through the streets of San Francisco.

David was at the finish line as she crossed, laughing, crying, falling exhausted into his arms.

Lee was there, standing over him, in the rain and darkness, when he stumbled in pain, clutching his left knee.

CHAPTER THREE

The plane parked at the main terminal and David spotted the tall, thin figure of his brother-in-law standing by the side of the exit.

Tom looked pretty much the same. Same baggy clothes and his shoulders slumped. Understandable.

Tom recognized David. "Here, give me that bag." David felt awkward as he let the bag slip from his hand. Tom started to walk and then, turned to put his arm around David's shoulder.

"Oh, God, what can I say? I'm so sick and alone."

"I know. I understand."

They exited the airport and started the drive on the Dulles Access Road toward Vienna.

"Tom, I made reservations at the Marriott in Vienna. I just thought it would be better that way."

"Okay, we can stop there now and you can check in and leave your things. Then we'll go home."

After David registered, they drove without speaking through the streets of Vienna. The city experienced a major building boom with the development of Tyson's Corners, the prosperous mall and business complex just to the east. Although a bedroom community, Vienna retained its southern atmosphere — tree-lined streets and houses set back on spacious lots, young trees growing on the groomed lawns. They arrived at a colonial brick townhouse on the outskirts of town, set on a cul de sac in a new development. Tom unlocked the front door and they stepped into a room lit from paned windows. David thought he detected the faint fragrance of his sister's cologne.

"A cup of coffee?"

"Yes, thanks. Hot and black will work," David said. He slumped in a chair, fatigued from the flight and lack of sleep, and surveyed the room — the dining table with silver candlesticks, an embroidered linen tablecloth, the pictures on the wall. He could sense his sister's hand in the decor. Yes, of course, the candlesticks, their mother's.

Tom poured two cups of coffee and then sat across from David. "How to begin?" he said, more to himself than to David. "I'm going to be honest with you. I'll try to explain everything, but there'll be things you can't understand and I can't explain." He stopped and rubbed his eyes. "Just keep one thing in mind. I loved your sister more than life."

David didn't respond for a moment. "How long have you and Lee lived here?"

Tom looked at him, seeming to be interrupted in his train of thought. "Oh, about three months. Yes, we moved here about three months ago."

David drank his coffee. "Okay, didn't mean to interrupt."

"I'm one of a small group of scientists working on a classified project, a medical project involving brain-stem tissue. This tissue comes from aborted fetuses, you know, a big political issue over its use. Nevertheless, the implications for breakthroughs are enormous. Hence, the ultra secrecy. We dispersed into small units throughout the country and the staff floated between the units in order to coordinate the work. That's why we moved so often."

David interrupted. "My only sister is dead. I want to know right now how she died."

Tom hesitated and turned away. "She killed herself. Overdosed on sleeping pills."

"Oh, my God." David placed his hands over his face, fingers massaging the throbbing in his forehead. "Why? How could such a thing happen? I don't understand what you're saying?"

Tom walked to a desk in a corner of the room and picked up a sheet of paper, which he handed to David.

My dearest Tom,

I know I have hurt you terribly and I didn't want to do this because I love you so much. But, I just can't go on like this. I want to be with my babies and have peace. Try and understand and forgive me.

Lee

David stared at his sister's handwriting and reread the note. "I don't understand," he said after several minutes of silence. "What did she mean about 'going on like this'? You didn't have any children. What did she mean about 'her babies?' What the hell does all this mean?"

Tom walked over to David and put his hand on his shoulder. "I'll try to explain in a way that will make some sense." He picked up the coffee cups, left them on the sink and returned to his chair. When he sat, his shoulders slumped and he sighed before beginning.

"We wanted to have children, but each time the fetuses aborted. We tried in-vitro fertilization, which seemed promising, but the fertilized egg never developed in her uterus."

"She aborted it, also?"

"No."

"No. No what?" The pitch of David's voice began to rise. "She didn't abort it, so what happened?" He grabbed Tom's arm as if to arouse a response. "What happened?"

"It just stayed there, inside her, living but not developing. It stopped growing."

David fumbled for his chair, sat down, and threw his head back, staring at the ceiling, trying to comprehend, to piece together in some meaningful way what he was being told. Too tired and grief-stricken, he couldn't cope with it, now. He realized that he'd have to cross-examine Tom, pull the bits and pieces from him to understand what happened. There would have to be time later for this.

"What about funeral arrangements?" David said. "When can I see her?"

"She was cremated this morning. That was her wish."

CHAPTER FOUR

David entered his room at the Marriott and fell on the bed, exhausted. He could have stayed longer with Tom, but he needed to be alone and private for a while. Tom's explanation about the project and Lee's death confused him, but he knew there had to be a link. At least that much Tom made clear. He'd shower, sleep, and then press Tom for details.

I don't want to be told that I can't understand. I will understand.

His sleep was restless with nightmares. He and Lee were running along the Ridge Trail on the crest of the East Bay Hills at Inspiration Point. The evening was getting dark. As they passed through the eucalyptus grove, some two miles from the car, he heard her call.

She had been on his right side, somewhat back, but keeping stride. He couldn't see her, of course, but he sensed her presence. He heard a cry. Stopped, and turned around but she wasn't there. He shouted, "Lee." His voice reverberated through the darkness. "Lee, where are you?"

Silence. The darkness crept in with trepidation. He was alone. His muscles ached. Could he make it back? His left knee began to ache.

Why was he thinking about himself? Where was his sister? Lost in the darkness? "Lee, where are you?"

His voice echoed back from the night.

David pulled himself up in bed and wiped the sweat beads from his upper lip. Shutting his eyes, he pictured his sister smiling at him. But she was dead.

David Green was a man of habit. He started to straighten the sheets and blankets, then smiled, realizing he was in a motel. At the closet, he unzipped the garment bag the bellboy had unfolded and hung when David checked in. He inspected his gray suit for wrinkles, and satisfied that it met his criteria, neared the dresser where he chose a white shirt, maroon tie, fresh underwear, handkerchief, and black socks to match his black shoes. He undressed, folded his pajamas and placed them in the top dresser drawer. Following his shower, David dressed, took a quick swipe with his socks across the polished top of his shoes before slipping them on, and finished dressing by tying his tie so it hung just below his belt. Now prepared for the business of the day, David walked to the motel coffee shop with the morning paper he'd found outside his door. Small orange juice, coffee and dry toast. When finished he paid the check, exited the motel, and hailed a taxi to Tom's house.

The sun was bright in a cloudless sky as the fall wind scattered leaves. David sat back in his seat, confident that today he would get the answers to his questions. The memory of his dream lay in a distant corner of his mind. As the taxi turned to Tom's street, David bolted forward in his seat, knees pressing into the crease of his pants, for a Mayflower moving van was backed into Tom's driveway and he could see men loading furniture from the house. He paid the cab driver and half ran to the front door.

"Is Dr. Osborne here?" he asked a worker leaving with a chair in his arms.

"Nobody here." The worker continued toward the truck.

David stood watching the workers as sweat curled down his neck into his shirt collar. He entered the house and searched through the rooms, avoiding men packing crates and cartons. Finding no clue, he left the house and approached a man entering data onto a sheet attached to a clipboard.

"Excuse me. Are you in charge here? Do you know where the owner is, Dr. Osborne?"

The man looked up from his work. "Afraid not. We're just the movers."

"Where are you moving this to?"

"Into storage. That's all I know. You can call the company if you want more details. Number is on the side of the truck." The man resumed checking the inventory of items being loaded.

David reentered the house, avoiding movers who ignored him, and walked into the room that had been Tom's office. Desk, computer, and books had all been either removed or stored in cartons.

Goddamit, how could I have screwed up?

His fingernails dug into his clenched fists.

Why did I leave him alone?

David slumped against a wall and brushed his hair back from his forehead as he realized he didn't know where Tom worked.

If only I'd gotten off my ass and come over here earlier.

David didn't know what to do. A mover pushed a dolly into the room, loaded several cartons of books, and left. The cartons had blocked a phone, which had sat on a desk now gone. The phone rested on the floor, cord still connected to the wall outlet so, picking up the phone, David put the receiver to his ear and heard the dial tone. He sat down on the floor with his knees drawn up, and placed the phone between his legs on the floor. He tore off a section of wrapping paper from a lamp, withdrew a pen from his shirt pocket, held his breath, and hit the redial button.

"Jefferson Research," a voice answered.

"Dr. Tom Osborne, please."

After several seconds the voice said, "Dr. Osborne isn't here. Is there a message I can leave for him?"

"No, thanks. It's not important. Tell me, please, what's your address?"

"We're in the Franklin Building at Tyson's II. Is there anything else I can do for you? Can I have your name?"

"Thank you. You've been very helpful."

Alan J. Gould

CHAPTER FIVE

In the seventies, Tyson's Corners was just a shopping center on the south side of Rt. 123 at its intersection with Rt. 7 in the Northern Virginia suburbs of Washington. Most of the commercial activity was centered at Seven Corners, some seven or eight miles south of Tyson's Corners. In the nineties, however, Tyson's exploded in growth expanding north across the highway and encompassing a massive development of commercial complexes housing research and defense related enterprises doing business with the federal government. The somewhat sleepy, rural area became an integral and vital component of the greater Washington dynamic of industry and government.

David's taxi wound through the maze of streets and buildings comprising Tyson's II. The expanse of modern buildings of glass and chrome was a model of planned development. The taxi pulled into a circular drive leading to a three-story building set back from the highway. The sign in front read, "Jefferson Research Inc. Franklin Building."

He strode through the glass doors of the entrance, bypassing sets of chairs, sofas, and tables at both his right and left, and moved ahead to an oval desk where two receptionists sat. Behind the reception desk and to the right, were more glass doors leading into the interior. David noticed access through these doors was gained either by swiping an identity card through a sensor or by the receptionists utilizing a buzzer release. People, no doubt employees, entered the building using their identity cards, which most wore on chains around their necks. Three or four individuals waited in the reception area, one or two drinking coffee from plastic cups obtained from a coffee station in an alcove off the reception area. Above the reception desk, in a chrome frame, hung an impressionistic painting of the Great Falls of the Potomac, just north of Washington.

David approached the desk and stood behind a young woman ahead of him. Rather tall, she was perhaps 5'10" or so, almost as tall as he. Dressed in a suit with a single strand of pearls over a black sweater, she appeared to be almost his age, perhaps twenty-eight or twenty-nine, trim and cute.

The closest receptionist smiled. "How can I help you?"

"I'm here to see Dr. Osborne,"

She smiled back. Surprised by this exchange, David moved to the left rear of the receptionist.

"Was Dr. Osborne expecting you?" the receptionist asked.

"No, it's a surprise. I'm his daughter."

David bit the inside of his lower lip and had to overcome an impulse to interject, "His daughter? That's not true. She couldn't be his daughter." He closed his eyes and held his hands together to keep from trembling.

"May I have your full name please, Ms. Osborne?"

"Sheila. Sheila Osborne."

"Please take a seat. Have a cup of coffee. The station is to your left. I'll be with you shortly."

The receptionist pressed a button under her desk that released the interior glass doors, arose, and walked through. The doors shut and locked behind her.

The young woman chose a chair behind a low table with magazines so David selected a chair in the same cluster and picked up a magazine. He could observe her now, pretty, not beautiful, her face, perhaps a little too angular, high cheekbones and thin lips. Her most striking features, however, were her eyes. David had known people with those intense, pale blue eyes that are somehow hard to avoid. They seem to penetrate one's thoughts. Hers had an added characteristic, a violet hue, as if flecks of violet dust swept across the surface. She glanced at him. He lowered his glance to the magazine, and sucked on his sore lower lip as he tried to relate her features with those of his brother-in-law. Tom was tall and angular. She certainly could have inherited that from him, but the face and those eyes. Obviously, she couldn't be Tom's daughter. Tom was, perhaps, a few years older than he, maybe thirty-seven, thirty-eight. This woman was in her late twenties. Even if she were in her early twenties, how could she be the daughter of Tom? There was something very wrong.

The receptionist returned through the glass doors with a man dressed in a gray business suit.

"I understand that you're looking for Dr. Osborne, Miss."

She glanced up, then stood where she could look him in the eyes. "I'm his daughter. I want to see him."

For a brief moment, the man returned her gaze, then averted his eyes.

"He isn't here, Ms. Osborne. When I hear from him I'll tell him you were here. Are you staying in town?"

She ignored his question. "When will he be back?"

"All I can tell you, believe me, is I don't know when or if Dr. Osborne will return. He has left this facility. If I hear from him, I'll certainly tell him you were here."

David had difficulty swallowing. He wiped his forehead with his handkerchief and blew his nose. He rose and stood between Ms. Osborne and the man.

"I couldn't help overhearing your conversation," David said. "I'm also looking for Dr. Osborne. I'm his brother-in-law."

Both the young woman and the man turned toward David in surprise. Before either could respond, David continued. "Does he work here or not? If he doesn't when did he leave? I was with him yesterday and he gave no indication he was leaving town. I want to know where he is."

The man backed away. "I'm sorry but you must appreciate my position. I couldn't reveal that type of information to anyone even if I had it. The best I can do is take your cards, or your names. You must excuse me."

He retreated through the glass doors, swiping the identification strip on the card that hung on a chain around his neck.

Aware that it was futile to argue with the receptionist, David took a business card from his coat pocket as the woman, Sheila Osborne, withdrew a card from her purse and handed it over. Nothing more was said. They exited the building, not quite together. When they reached the curb, she turned to David. "Would you mind telling me who the hell you are and why you said you're my father's brother-in-law?"

He was glad she initiated the conversation.

"Look," he struggled for words. "I'm sorry I startled you and I didn't mean to upset you. You said you're his daughter. Believe me when I tell you, you startled me because I have a hard time understanding. I think we have to talk. Are you from out of town?"

She paused a long moment before responding. "I'm at the Key Bridge Marriott. Meet me in the lobby at noon."

Without waiting for an answer, she climbed into a waiting cab and through an opened window called out, "My name is Sheila."

"And mine is David," he shouted back but he couldn't be certain she heard him.

CHAPTER SIX

In his hotel room, David inspected his lower lip in the bathroom mirror. The action caused a trickle of blood to ooze out. He spat into the sink.

Dammit, I screwed up royally. Tom must have decided on all of this when I was with him. As soon as I was out of sight he must have called the movers and pulled this vanishing act. And who the hell is this woman who says she's his daughter? What is she up to?

He thought again of his sister. The knowledge that she was gone forever gave rise to feelings of loneliness and despair. Their parents had died while they were young so Lee became mother as well as older sister. Now David no longer had a family. Sadness compounded the simmering anger he felt over the mystery of her death.

He looked at his watch. Less than an hour to meet Sheila Osborne. What to do? Check out and make reservations to fly back to San Francisco or wait to see what transpires from meeting with her. He'd wait.

In the lobby of the Key Bridge Marriott, David saw Sheila Osborne seated at a corner table. She nodded to him and beckoned him to sit down. She had changed clothes, he noticed, into black slacks and a white sweater. When he was seated across from her, she announced, "I've checked out and am going home. I give up. There's nothing more I can do here."

"Where is home?" David said.

"Albany."

Awkward and not certain what to say, he replied. "I'm from San Francisco."

A pause ensued.

"What's your last name, David?"

"Green. David Green. I'm an attorney in private practice in Emeryville. That's just across the Bay Bridge from San Francisco. And you?"

"Physical therapist, but let's get to your relationship with my father. You say you're his brother-in-law. He's married to your sister?"

David leaned back in his chair and sensed again the reality of his loss.

"I came here because my sister died. She only died two days ago and yet it seems like ages with all that has happened."

His hand slid under the table to touch his left knee as if anticipating a surge of pain.

Sheila Osborne's face softened. "Everything seems so sad and confusing. I can't seem to find my father and you lost your sister. I'm sorry to hear that, really."

She reached over and squeezed his hand.

"You're very nice," he said, "but I wonder if we're talking about the same man, I mean, your father and my brother-in-law."

"I don't understand." Her body seemed to stiffen in defense.

"Well, I mean, do you have an older brother? Tom junior?" He hadn't intended to antagonize or alienate her, so he implored, "Listen, please, and don't get angry with me, at least not yet. My sister, Lee, was thirty-three and, Tom, well I never actually knew his age but I guess around thirty-seven."

"My father is fifty-eight and no, I don't have a brother," she replied in a crisp voice. "Here, let me show you something."

From her purse Sheila withdrew a photograph. Although somewhat stained, it showed a man holding the hand of a little girl at Disneyland.

"That's my father and me. I was five."

David stared at the photograph of his brother-in-law, who looked exactly the same in the picture as he did yesterday. Shaken, David handed the photograph back to Sheila.

Who was this man who was married to my sister? What did I really know about him? Oh yes, he had all the right credentials — good looking, educated, and she loved him. What else mattered? All the secrecy — government projects, classified? I never questioned anything. Why should I? What business was it of mine anyway? Lee was happy. Wasn't she?

"Well," Sheila said, "are we talking about the same person?"

"Please listen to me. I'm not the enemy. Trust me. I want to find my brother-in-law because there are things about my sister's death I don't know and want to clear up. You're looking for your father. In short, perhaps we may be looking for the same person. Perhaps we can help each other. Will you give it a try?"

She hesitated, only a moment, before answering him. "Why not? What have I got to lose? I'm here already. First, let me see if I can catch a later flight and then let's have lunch."

He couldn't help but notice how the violet flecks cast an aura around her eyes when she smiled.

The dining room of the Key Bridge Marriot had large windows overlooking the Potomac River. The spires of Georgetown University could be seen rising above the waterfront of chic restaurants and shops. David Green and Sheila Osborne sat at a table for two in a corner with a view of the city.

"We both have questions," he began. "Tom Osborne is the only person who can give us answers. Let's work together to find him."

She stirred her tea and seemed to consider his suggestion. "What was your sister like? I mean, what did she look like? Tall? Blond?"

"Well, yes, in a way, I suppose." He shifted his weight in his chair. "No, she wasn't really blond. She had light brown hair, bangs in front and sort of straight, you know, not curly. Wore it back in a ponytail when she ran. Tied with a kerchief. She worked in a bookstore and was always trying to get me to go to one of those author's things, you know, they come to the store and have a reading. She wrote, also, poems and actually had a small book of poems published. I remember how she laughed when she told me about it. 'A great success. Only cost me three hundred dollars to get it printed.'"

"I'm sorry. I didn't mean to make you sad. I was just curious. I can see how very close you were to her."

"No, that's okay, really." He smiled and looked up at her. "Now it's your turn. Tell me about your father."

"I was young when he left. He always seemed so very tall and I loved it when he picked me up and put me on his shoulder. He called me Peanut and would pull my ponytail. I had a braided one then. He had such patience with me. In the evening he always found time to read to me, and answer my questions. Do you know the capital of Albania? I do. I knew all the capitals of Europe. I never understood why he left us. You can't imagine what it felt like."

David fingered the menu. "What would you like for lunch?"

"Tuna fish salad, and yes, I would like to work with you to find my father. I'm not sure what we can do but I'm willing to try anything."

"Good. I'm glad. I have a few ideas on where to start and we can go over them while we eat."

A man entered the dining area, paused, surveyed the room and walked to their table.

"Excuse me. Are you David Green and Sheila Osborne?"

Halting their conversation, they looked up at the stranger. He had the appearance of a businessman in his tailored gray suit, white, button-down shirt, and blue striped tie.

"Who are you?" David said.

"My name's Carson. I'm with the FBI."

From his coat pocket Carson produced credentials. David examined them, and studied the picture before returning them to Mr. Carson.

"How can we help you?" David said.

"My supervisor, John King, would like to talk to you about Dr. Osborne. We know you were both asking for him this morning and perhaps we can assist. Mr. King would like to meet you at his office. I can take you there."

"What do you think?" David said to Sheila. "Do you have time before your plane leaves?"

She checked her watch. "Sure. If I miss it, what the hell. What have we got to lose?"

They followed Mr. Carson outside where he held open the rear door of a dark blue Buick sedan for them.

David could always tell a government car. No trim and a smell like antiseptic.

Mr. Carson drove across the Potomac on the Roosevelt Bridge onto Virginia Avenue. He swung into the oval driveway leading to the Watergate complex and pulled into a parking spot marked "Reserved." He led them to a suite on the sixth floor, and a reception room furnished with a leather sofa and several matching leather chairs around a mahogany and glass table. A Persian rug covered the floor. A bronze lamp with three arms holding flame-shaped bulbs under a silken shade lit the room.

"I'll let Mr. King know you're here." Mr. Carson left through a door leading into the next room.

"Pretty snazzy quarters." Sheila ran her hand over the leather of her chair.

"Not like any government office I've been in," David answered.

They didn't speak a word until Mr. Carson returned and guided them through the door, down a hallway, and past several rooms in which people were working at desks or meeting in conferences. David and Sheila stepped into a large office containing a desk in one corner, an oval conference table, chairs, and a sofa in the same style as those in the reception area. Mr. King resembled a college professor, with a "I'm brilliant. I don't have to conform" look, dark, unruly hair falling over his ears, a tangled beard, a Patrick James suit that needed a pressing, and Bally shoes that could use a shine. He rose from behind the desk and came over to greet them.

"Thank you both for coming. Please have a seat." He pointed to the conference table. David wondered if he would offer to shake hands. He didn't. Mr. Carson left them alone.

"We know that you both want to find Dr. Osborne. We want to find him also, and we believe that, with your help, we can." Mr. King addressed Sheila, "Tell me, Ms. Osborne, when was the last time you saw or had any word from Dr. Osborne?"

Sheila turned to David. He nodded for her to answer the question.

"We would hear from him, periodically, I mean, my mother would get letters or calls after they separated. He'd write to me also, when I grew older. Sometimes he'd call. But I never saw him. I think the last I heard from him was two years ago. Right after my mother died. He called me and then wrote. That was how I knew about Jefferson Research. His letter was on their letterhead. I decided yesterday it was time to track him down.

"Your parents were divorced, weren't they?"

"Yes, about five years after he left."

"Do you know why your father left?"

Sheila started to speak, but stopped. She glanced at David for a moment, then turned to Mr. King. "I really don't know what that has to do with this." Her voice rose as she straightened herself in her chair. "Why are you looking for my father? Tell me what you know."

"I want to help you, Sheila "

"Miss Osborne."

"I'm sorry, Miss Osborne. I want to help, but I must have your cooperation. It's important. Do you know why your father left, how many years ago?"

"He left about twenty years ago. I was about eight, I think. No, I don't know why he left?"

"Was it another woman?"

"No."

"Did your mother ever discuss it with you?"

Sheila stood and pointed a finger at Mr. King. "Look, I don't know where you're going with this but I'll answer you. No, my mother never discussed it with me, certainly not in any detail. She only told me that they were separating, that he loved me, and I probably wouldn't see him very much. That was it. Now you tell me. Where is my father?"

Mr. King didn't move from his chair. He spoke in a soft voice. "I told you, Miss Osborne, I don't know where your father is. If I did, I would tell you. Your information may be valuable, so again I ask for your cooperation. Please sit down."

Sheila turned and spoke to David. "I don't know where this patronizing S.O.B is going but my patience is wearing very thin." But she did return to her chair.

"After your mother died, Ms. Osborne, did you, perhaps, read any of your father's letters or her notes? Anything that might have given you a clue as to his work, or their separation, or anything like that?"

"No."

"No what? There were no letters or notes, or you didn't read them, or they didn't contain any information?"

"No to all of the above, and I think that's it. I'm ready to leave, David." She started to get up when Mr. King interjected.

"Please Miss Osborne. I'm sorry if I upset you. Let me ask you one last question."

Sheila Osborne stood across the table from Mr. King. "All right, one question."

From the files on the table in front of him, Mr. King withdrew a picture and handed it to Sheila. "Do you know this woman?"

She stared at the black and white photograph, full face, of a woman, perhaps in her mid-forties, dark eyes, framed by tortoise shell glasses, and staring straight at the camera. Sheila sat down again, her eyes fixed on the picture.

"Yes, it's Aunt Ruth."

"When was the last time you saw this woman, Aunt Ruth you called her?" Mr. King leaned forward on the conference table.

"Yes, Aunt Ruth. She worked with my father and came to our home for dinner once in a while. She was friends with my mother. What has she got to do with this?"

"When was the last time you saw her or heard from her?"

"I don't know, before my mother died, but I can't remember just when."

"Did you see her after your father left?"

Sheila rose from her chair, tossed the picture on the table and said to David, "I'm leaving here now. This is going no place. Are you coming with me?" David took the picture and examined it.

"Mr. King, who is this woman and what has she to do with this case?"

"Her name is Ruth Goldman, Dr. Goldman. She was an associate of Dr. Osborne. Do you know her, Mr. Green? Did Dr. Osborne or your sister ever refer to her?"

"I'm beginning to share Miss Osborne's impatience. No, I don't know this Dr. Goldman. Unless you can tell us what we came here to find out, I think we'll leave. We both have planes to catch." David beckoned to Sheila to start toward the door.

Mr. King crossed to the door and turned, facing them, back to the door.

"I want you to understand me very clearly." His voice rose and his face reddened. "If you know anything about Dr. Goldman, you are best advised to tell me now…anything and everything you know. Even if you are not sure of something, I want to hear it. Do I make myself clear?"

David approached Mr. King, standing close, emphasizing his height so that King had to look up to see his face.

"No, sir, you don't make yourself clear. Not at all. The only thing you make clear is that you seem to be threatening us and I don't like that. I don't know what's going on here. Hardly seems like an FBI office, but frankly I don't care. Now please get out of our way so we can leave."

"You can go now," Mr. King responded as he took two calling cards from his pocket and handed one to each of them. "If you hear from Dr. Osborne or Dr. Goldman I want you to call me, immediately."

As David put the card in his pocket, Sheila took hers, tore it up and threw it at King's feet. "I can't think of one reason why I would help you."

"Don't be so sure of yourself, Miss Osborne," Mr. King replied. "Remember what I said. If you find something or think of something I should know, I expect you to call me at once. If you don't, I assure you'll be very sorry, and that is definitely a threat. Goodbye."

Neither spoke as Mr. Carson drove them back to the Key Bridge Marriott. They went into the cocktail lounge and ordered drinks. Sheila glanced at her watch.

"I've about an hour and a half before my flight. My luggage is checked here and I guess it shouldn't take more than a half hour to National, so I do have a little time." She paused as if searching for words. "David, I just can't figure it out. What do you make of that whole episode?"

"I'm as much in the dark as you. That guy King really got to me. He angered me but, I must admit, he frightened me a little, too. I've never seen anything like that set-up." He took a drink. "What was all that about, Dr. Goldman?"

"Search me. I told him the truth. She worked with Dad and came to our house every so often. She wasn't married, as far as I know, and she sort of doted on me. You know, cute little girl. She'd bring me little gifts, candy. I called her Auntie Ruth. I think she liked that. There really isn't anything else to tell. I can't see the connection between her and my father's disappearance."

"Obviously they were much more interested in her than in him. I'm at a loss, also. I wish I had an idea what to do next, but I don't, so I think the best thing for us is to go home. Let's just keep in touch and see what happens."

Sheila reached over and took his hand in hers.

"David, I want you to know I'm glad we met and I'm sorry it was under these circumstances. I'm also sorry about your sister. Have a safe trip home."

Long flights are disassociated experiences. The individual is suspended between the time and events of the place he left and his destination. The clock starts running when the plane lands and the individual again assumes his persona, expectations, and responsibilities. For that interlude, however, time is suspended.

The night flight, backward in time, gained three hours into San Francisco. Most passengers were sleeping. He tilted his seat back and looked out the window. Total blackness. He shut his eyes and once again saw his sister's image. The last time he saw her was perhaps three or four months before. She'd come to California to see him, check on some business. She seemed happy. He searched his memory for some hint of trouble but it wasn't there. Was I so wrapped up in my own life that I missed some signal? Why did she kill herself? Why couldn't she have called me?

He tried to recall other images of her, like when the wind blew against her face, or how her ponytail stretched out behind her as she ran down the path.

As long as we keep running we're immortal.

As the images faded, David's thoughts turned to Sheila Osborne. He wondered if she, too, could run with the wind. He couldn't capture that image, but specks of violet, sparkling in the darkness of the night sky, floated through his mind.

CHAPTER SEVEN

On Sheila Osborne's uneventful flight to Albany, she thought about her father and the happy images of childhood now darkened by doubts. She recalled her mother explaining her father's absence. "He's away on a business trip, a long trip and we won't be seeing him for quite a while." At the time that seemed to make sense, but not now. She framed the questions she'd like to ask her mother today, pinning her down, demanding specifics. She'd tried to understand the compulsion that drove her to search for her father, to track him down, but what would she have said to him if he had walked through the glass doors at the Jefferson Institute? She realized the search was more a consequence of her own dissociated unease with her life, than a driven need to find her father.

The only thing that ever changed in her life was she grew older every day.

She picked up her car at the airport and drove into Albany, turned from New Scotland Avenue right onto South Main, and parked in the driveway of the house where she'd lived with her mother. She sat, staring at the two-story, white frame house, surrounded by a wide front porch and its two weathered rocking chairs with faded pillows beside a low wooden table.

The house needed a paint job, a face-lift.

Sheila and her mother used to sit on the porch, on hot summer nights, drinking iced tea and watching heat-lightning streak the sky.

This is my home now, all mine. My refuge. Refuge? What kind of word was that? Refuge from what?

She sighed, opened the car door and climbed up the four wooden steps with her overnight bag. She crossed the porch, inserted the door key into the lock, and turned it counter clock-wise. The bolt didn't retract. She placed her bag down, and pursed her lips as she jiggled the key forcing the bolt back. The door opened. As she withdrew the key, she noticed scratches on the face of the lock. She flipped the light switch. A flood of light revealed a scene of total chaos. Pillows and cushions from the chairs and sofa were strewn on the floor. Newspapers, notes, letters from her desk lay in piles. Books had been scattered, as if thrown to the ceiling in bunches and allowed to fall free. A table lamp had fallen on its side, bulb broken, the shards peppered on the lampshade where it had landed on the floor.

Sheila set her overnight bag down, and picked up the lampshade. As she held the shade, tears welled in her eyes. She placed the shade on the table by the lamp and continued into her bedroom. Every drawer of her dresser was open. She picked up a nightgown hanging half out of one drawer. Her underclothes had been twisted into heaps, some tossed on the floor. She clenched her fists and wiped the tears from the corners of her eyes.

"Those sons of bitches," she said out loud. "I won't be raped like this."

Sheila gathered her clothes from her hamper and carried them to the washing machine in the garage. Then she cleared the papers and pillows from the floor. Once the rooms were in order, she began rearranging papers at her desk. There she found the search warrant authorizing the FBI search of her home and the receipt for items seized — her mother's diary, pictures of her mother and father, her mother's letters, some notes, other documents. She folded the search warrant and receipt, and stuck them in a corner of the desk. Then she leaned back, shut her eyes and took a deep breath. When she opened her eyes she noticed her bag was still near the door where she'd dropped it. She started toward the bag, past the china cabinet, then stopped.

The china cabinet. The crystal glasses, china dishes, cups, saucers were all in place, untouched. Her lips curled into a tight smile. The damned fools missed it.

Sheila boiled water, poured it into a china teapot to which she added a tablespoon of loose tea. When the tea had steeped, she poured it into a glass of ice and carried it outside where she chose to sit in one of the rockers on the front porch. The leaves of the maple tree in front of the house rustled in a slight breeze. They had begun to turn, and the yellows and reds reflected off the streetlight in the semi-darkness. She stared at the empty rocker.

How long am I going to stay in this empty house with the ghost of my mother?

She sipped her tea, sat the glass on the small table, leaned back in the rocker, ran her fingers through her hair and watched fallen leaves drift up the empty street.

I think I'll call David tomorrow.

CHAPTER EIGHT

Emeryville lies on the eastern shore of San Francisco Bay midway between Oakland and Berkeley. Until recently, Emeryville was a site for small manufacturing and related businesses. However, since the boom in real estate values in the Bay Area, Emeryville became a prized location for high tech firms. This resulted in a building frenzy of office and apartment complexes with their malls abutting the depressed older neighborhoods.

David's apartment was on the fourteenth floor of an apartment building within walking distance of his office. He liked the view from his balcony overlooking the Bay. In the evening, he often sat there looking at the lights of San Francisco and watching the sun set over the Golden Gate Bridge.

In the past, when the summer afternoons were hot, he'd get up early and run from his apartment to the Emeryville marina, past the berthed boats and apartments, to the park at the water's edge, and then back. He still ran the same five miles, but slower now. With his damaged knee he had to make a conscious effort to shorten his stride, to rein himself in. If he listened to the doctor's repeated advice, he wouldn't be running at all. But it was impossible for him to give up such an important part of his life. Although he realized his marathon days were over, the reality was hard to accept. So he compromised. He knew he'd need a knee replacement if he kept running, even at a slow pace, and at shortened distances. He buried that reality deep at the back of his mind.

Following his return from Washington, David knew he wouldn't run that morning or later. He tossed back and forth under the covers, his mind racing in disorganized images.

What was it he overheard between Lee and Tom when he last saw them together? Did she say she wanted to see a doctor? Why didn't she call me? Did she kill herself?

David opened his eyes to the dim light of dawn coming through the window and didn't want to move. His arms and legs were heavy and the knee, that damn left knee, was stiff. With some effort he showered, dressed and decided to drive rather than walk to his office. Marina, his secretary and office manager, had coffee brewing when he arrived. He was glad to see a friend.

"You look terrible. What happened?"

"Lee is dead, Marina."

Her hand shook as she placed her coffee cup on her desk. Then put her arms around him.

"My God, that's terrible. Poor Lee. Dead?" Tears filled her eyes.

David didn't answer but walked into his office. Marina had stacked his mail in a neat pile. His telephone message slips sat by the telephone. He looked up at Marina standing in the doorway. "Bring your coffee in and sit down. I'll tell you what I know." David had no hesitation in sharing his feelings with Marina. She'd been his friend and confidant since he hired her three years before. With an unspoken understanding their personal lives were separate.

She listened and when he was through, she said, "What are you going to do?"

"I honestly don't know, yet. I need time to think this through."

"Maybe you could call Corey Tenet. He's a good friend. Perhaps he could get some information about that FBI operation."

David smiled at her. "You always come up with the answer, don't you?"

Corey Tenet, a deputy U. S. Attorney in San Francisco, had been David's classmate. Their friendship continued after graduation. A good trial lawyer, not a flamboyant spellbinder, he was meticulous in researching the law and facts of every case, and had earned a respected reputation in the bar.

David decided not to go into detail with Corey, but ask if he could get a line on John King. Early morning was the best time to find Corey at the office. After explaining his case involved a Washington D. C. office of the FBI headed by a John King, he gave Corey the telephone number and address from the card King had given him.

"I should be able to get some fix on this right away," Corey said. "I'll make some calls this morning. But there's a price for this. I think it's your turn to buy lunch. Trader Vic's at noon?"

"I think it's your turn, Corey, but I won't argue. T.V.'s at noon. See you there."

David knew Corey liked an excuse to cross the Bay Bridge for lunch with him at Trader Vic's near the marina in Emeryville, world famous for its seafood and island dishes.

One look at Corey and David knew something was wrong. Corey had a habit of clapping David on the back with a "hail fellow" greeting, but today he remained still. Somewhat shorter than David, Corey looked into David's eyes with a perplexed expression. He didn't smile as he took out his handkerchief and dabbed his forehead where the hairline had begun to recede.

"What the hell kind of thing are you involved in, David?" But without waiting for an answer, Corey followed the maitre'd to a corner table overlooking the Bay. After they ordered drinks and lunch, Corey leaned forward.

"You asked about John King. Well, this guy is something very special. The only thing I can tell you about him is he's way up. I mean way up. Every time I asked for details I was shut down. I've never seen anything like it. You'd think I was asking for missile launch codes. What the hell is this all about?"

David took a drink, then regarded his friend. "I do owe you an explanation, but before I begin, I want you to know that I've done nothing wrong, and I hope you don't get into trouble because of this."

For the first time, Corey smiled. "I won't get into any trouble. So don't worry about me. Tell me, for Christ's sake, what's going on?"

David related the details beginning with his brother-in-law's phone call, his meeting with Sheila Osborne, and their meeting with John King.

"I don't know what else I can tell you. I don't know what to make of this. That's why I called you. I thought if I had some information, some idea what this is all about, I might know what to do. I'm at a loss."

Corey didn't respond. Minus their usual conversation David and Corey ate their lunch and then ordered coffee. After David paid the check, they started toward the entrance when Corey took David's arm and stopped him.

"Listen to me...carefully." He paused and lowered his voice. "Be very careful about your telephone conversations. Now, forget you heard that from me."

David rested his hand on his friend's shoulder.

"Thanks, buddy, you're a real friend."

Corey wiped his forehead with his handkerchief and then blew his nose. "Just be careful, David." He turned and got into his car the parking attendant had driven to the entrance.

At his office, and once more at his desk, David began to sort through the telephone messages.

"How did it go with Corey?" Marina said, pausing in the doorway.

"He couldn't tell me very much. But he said he'd check further and let me know. Anything doing here?"

"You got one call, a Sheila Osborne. Here's the number."

He closed the office door and dialed. He hadn't expected to hear from her, at least so soon, but he was glad she'd called.

"It's David. How are you?" he said as soon as she answered.

"The truth is, I'm extremely angry. Those bastards searched my house before I came home. You wouldn't believe what it looked like. I think they went out of their way to mess my things up."

"My God, that's terrible. Did they have a warrant? Did they take anything?"

"They had a warrant all right. Left a copy of it with a receipt for the things they took. All my mother's letters, notes, and some of my correspondence. I have an appointment with a lawyer tomorrow, a friend of mine, to see about getting my things back. But that's not what I called about."

"Well, I'm glad that you're all right and I'm sorry you had to go through all this. Tell me, how can I help?"

Sheila's voice changed from tones of anger to excitement. "You know they were looking for anything involving Aunt Ruth. I still don't have a clue why they want her so badly, but the damn fools missed it."

David straightened in his chair and pressed the phone close to his mouth. He spoke in a whisper. "What do you mean they missed it?"

"The idiots ransacked my house, threw my underwear on the floor and missed the one thing they were looking for. It was sitting in plain view in my china closet. I have it right here."

He didn't respond. The second hand on the desk clock ticked off twenty seconds.

"David, did you hear me?"

"Don't say another word. Not a word. Listen to me carefully. Your phone is tapped. They're hearing everything we say." He looked at his watch. "It's about four-thirty in Albany, right?"

"I don't understand." Her voice seemed apprehensive.

"Sheila, do you trust me?"

"Yes."

"I mean really trust me?"

"Yes, I do. I really trust you. What do you want me to do?"

"I'm not completely sure. I must think this out as I speak. We don't have time, Sheila. They're on their way to your house right now. You must leave. It's late in the day so you probably have around fifteen or twenty minutes to clear out. Understand?"

"Yes. But what do I do then? Where do I go?"

"Let me think." The second hand on the clock continued its circle. "You remember the picture you showed me? The one of you and your Dad when you were little?

"Yes."

"Good. We'll meet at the place where the picture was taken. Don't mention the place. Remember, they're listening. Do you understand?"

"Yes, but…"

"Listen to me. Leave this minute. Take a few things and clear out. Go to a branch of your bank. Withdraw as much cash as you can. Go to a close friend whom you trust. Exchange cars. That will throw them off for a while. Take buses, drive, take planes, trains. Keep changing until you get to the place in the picture. Remember, planes are dangerous because they require picture ID and you can be traced. Don't use credit cards. Get out and go right now. Any questions?"

"David, I'm scared. But I'll do what you say and don't worry. I'll see you there, you know where. Goodbye."

"I'm on my way, also. See you soon."

He sat back in his chair and stared at his trembling hands. Jesus Christ, what did I do? He felt he couldn't move, couldn't command his legs to stand him up. He knew he must move. David put his head back against his chair and shut his eyes. He tried to picture his sister hoping her image would energize him to move, to get going, start running. He opened his eyes and looked at his watch. Five minutes had passed since his conversation with Sheila.

Could they be at the entrance of his building already? Are they on the way up the stairs and the elevator?

He rose from his chair, slipped on his suit coat, and opened his briefcase. He pulled his checkbook from the lower desk drawer and put three pages of checks in the briefcase before he opened the office door and approached Marina. "How much cash is on hand?" As if she could sense his nervousness, she didn't answer, but unlocked the petty cash box, withdrew all the bills and counted out about four hundred dollars.

"Give them to me and write a check for cash," he said. "I'll be gone for a while. Don't know exactly how long. I'll call and keep in touch."

"David, take care of yourself."

"I will. Don't worry about me." He left the office and headed for the Emeryville branch of Wells Fargo Bank located on the ground floor of his office building. He made a calculated judgment that he could be in and out of the bank before the agents arrived and because he knew the manager, he walked to her desk. She was talking with a customer, but saw David and acknowledged him with a smile. He settled into a chair, picked up a magazine and made the motions of thumbing through it as he kept an eye on the glass doors of the main entrance apprising each person who entered. He glanced at his watch. Thirteen minutes since the call from Sheila.

At last the customer left and Ms. Knight stood, smiled, and extended her hand.

"Mr. Green, nice to see you. What can I do for you?"

He explained he had to go on an emergency business trip and required as much cash as possible. David had both business and personal lines of credit as well as high checking account balances.

"Let me see what I can do for you." Ms. Knight entered his account numbers into her computer and read the data as it appeared. "You have over fifteen thousand dollars in your checking account. If you want to write a check for that amount I can handle that."

Withdrawing one of the blank checks from his briefcase he wrote the required check. He hoped she wouldn't see his hand shaking as he signed his name. She took the check, walked across the lobby and entered the area behind the tellers. David glanced at his watch. Twenty minutes since the call.

Soon Ms. Knight returned and counted out fifteen thousand dollars on her desktop. He signed the receipt she prepared, put the cash in his briefcase, thanked her with a smile, and left the bank. He hurried to his car, parked in the area reserved for tenants of the building, backed out of the parking slot, drove around the corner and parked. Breathing in gasps, he sat back in the seat, sweat dripping into his eyes and, as he wiped his forehead he congratulated himself on the fact that he drove instead of walked to work that morning.

Okay, so far. I have to be clever, follow the same advice I gave Sheila. Let me think. I can't get far in my car. Swap with a friend? He gave a short laugh. Not likely. Everyone's at work. Think, think, be clever, use your mind.

He had to assume that all airports, bus terminals, and train stations would soon be under surveillance.

I need to act and I need a plan, now.

The idea began to develop as he sat with the engine running. He released the brake and, as the plan solidified in his mind he began driving with a purpose. He stopped at a convenience store, purchased a copy of the daily paper, then drove toward the Oakland Airport. As he approached the "Long Term" parking lot he kept glancing into the rear-view mirror. Every car behind him might be the enemy. David could picture John King driving a black car, with King's agents closing in on him, cutting him off, and dragging him from his seat.

Didn't I warn you, Mr. Green?

David took the ticket from the dispensing machine, the gate opened and he drove into the lot, parked the car in the first available slot, took his briefcase and newspaper, locked the car and walked toward the terminal.

This is it. If they're going to get me it will be now.

He wanted to take the Bay Area Rapid Transit (BART) train, gambling that they couldn't deploy agents to all transportation terminals that soon. He tried to identify agents but realized it was impossible. He boarded the train, found a seat near the rear of the first car, unfolded the newspaper and held it high to cover his face. He tried to relax but his muscles were tense, his mouth dry. He licked his lips. The train left the airport without incident and David realized that he had been successful, so far.

David folded the paper to the classified section and began scanning the ads for used cars. He circled several ads, then refolded the paper and waited until the train reached the next station where he exited. At a telephone booth, he called the first circled ad. It required three calls before he reached a party who was available to show him a car right now. The seller lived in Fremont and agreed to meet David at the Fremont BART station. He checked the fare from a fare chart on the wall, purchased a ticket from one of the vending machines in the station, glanced around, then took the escalator to the train platform. The ten minutes it took the train to arrive seemed interminable to David. He sat in the last car and kept the newspaper close to his face.

The car was a five-year-old Honda Accord. He didn't know a great deal about cars but he examined the interior and exterior, and drove the car around the neighborhood. It seemed to have been well maintained. It shifted, braked and accelerated with ease and was clean. David negotiated a price with the owner and they drove back to the owner's home. David paid him in cash, had the owner sign the registration and title documents, shook hands, and left in his new car. At a gas station, he filled the tank and purchased a container of coffee and a tuna salad sandwich. Putting the coffee container in the receptacle between the seats he unwrapped the sandwich placing it in the paper bag on the passenger's seat. He smiled.

Alan J. Gould

So far so good. I'm smarter than they are.

He drove in the right hand lane, within the speed limit, and out Route 580 toward the intersection with Interstate 5 where he headed south toward Los Angeles.

CHAPTER NINE

The limousine stopped at the office entrance to the United States Supreme Court. Jeff Martin, the chauffeur, dressed in a leather jacket, white shirt, tie, and tan slacks, switched off the engine, and, at the curbside, leaned against the vehicle waiting for his charge, Justice Lawrence Crane Devon. Judge Devon had been on the court for eleven years, having been appointed during the last Republican administration. Raised in Montana, he gained a well-deserved reputation for his scholarship in the Montana courts and as a federal judge in the ninth circuit. He was considered conservative but not ideological, and his crafted, reasoned opinions carried considerable persuasive value in the inner court dialogues.

When Jeff Martin saw the tall, angular figure of the judge approach the limousine he opened the rear door, brought his fingers to his forehead in a semi-salute and greeted the judge. "Afternoon, your honor. Short day?"

"Afternoon, Jeff. Short day here but still things to be done." He entered the car. Jeff shut the door and returned to the driver's seat. No partition separated the front and rear seats for the judge had ordered it removed so he could be free to talk with the chauffeur who now said, "Where to, Judge?"

"Watergate Towers, main entrance. When you get there, leave me off and wait as I shouldn't be more than forty-five minutes to an hour or so."

Jeff headed the car west down Pennsylvania Avenue toward the Potomac River. Judge Devon leaned back and let his head rest against the soft leather. He shut his eyes for a few moments, and then stretched his hand beyond the cuff of his suit coat and read his watch — 4:00 p.m.

Good, let them stew for a while.

At 4:13, the limousine pulled up the crescent drive of the Watergate complex. Jeff shut off the engine and started to open his door. Instead, the Judge said. "Stay where you are, Jeff. I'll see you shortly." As he got out he smiled and Jeff gave him a half-salute.

The receptionist met Judge Devon at the door of the FBI suite and ushered him through the halls to the main conference room where John King and three agents rose from their chairs.

"Thank you for coming, your honor. Would you please sit at the head of the table?" John King beckoned the judge to the chair intended for him.

"You sit there, John. This is your conference." Judge Devon selected a chair at the side of the table. When the others took their places, Judge Devon turned to King, "Okay, now brief me."

"Your honor, first let me introduce my associates who have been directly involved in this case." To his right King indicated a short, balding man. "This is agent Carson. This is Agent McGee," and he indicated a slender man with graying hair. Agent McGee nodded to the judge and smiled. Judge Devon returned the smile. "This is Agent Fallon," and he pointed to a woman in her mid-thirties with straight brown hair pulled back and tied in a tight bun. She nodded to the judge.

John King cleared his throat and concentrated on the judge.

"Your honor, I'm afraid that our information is inconclusive. Each agent will give you a report specific to his or her assignment and each is prepared to elaborate in as much detail as you require. At this time, unfortunately, we don't have the locations of David Green, Sheila Osborne or Dr. Goldman. Our operations continue nationwide. I can't give you any reasonable estimate as to when we'll locate them. However, we will find them. They can't hide from us forever."

He paused but Judge Devon made no response. Mr. King motioned to Agent Carson. "Brief us on David Green."

Agent Carson put on his reading glasses and straightened the notes that sat in front of him.

"I believe your honor has seen a transcript of the telephone conversation between David Green and Sheila Osborne, which occurred in the afternoon of September seventeenth. Following the intercept, Agent Smith and I proceeded directly to his office in Emeryville from where the call had been placed. Emeryville is located on the eastern shore of San Francisco Bay near the approach to the Bay Bridge. We arrived at approximately four-fifteen. We…"

The judge interrupted. "What time was the call intercepted?"

Agent Carson seemed caught off guard for a moment. He reviewed his notes. "Approximately three twenty-four."

The judge waved his hand indicating Agent Carson should continue.

"His secretary stated that Mr. Green had left the office approximately a half hour before our arrival. We went to his apartment, also in Emeryville, but he wasn't there. We determined that he had taken flight and alerted headquarters for a general response, surveillance of all public transport systems, local police alert for his automobile, contact with his bank. We determined he had withdrawn over fifteen thousand dollars in cash."

"What time was that?"

"About four o'clock."

"So he had about an hour or so to empty his bank and bolt, right?"

"By five o'clock, your honor, we had agents dispersed throughout all the terminals in the Bay Area."

"And?" A tone of impatience accentuated the question.

"We found his car parked at Oakland Airport. This was at about eight p.m. We checked all out-going flights from Oakland from four o'clock on and are certain he wasn't on any of them."

"So what is your professional opinion as to where he is?"

Agent Carson didn't reply right away. He glanced at his associates, then breathed in, and said to the judge. "We don't know. He could've had a friend pick him up or loan him a car. He had suggested something like that to Ms. Osborne. We're checking his friends, but so far, no missing cars. Nothing."

Judge Devon turned his head away from Agent Carson. After a few moments Agent King motioned Agent McGee to start.

After scanning his notes and clearing his throat, McGee said, "My partner and I reached Ms. Osborne's home approximately one hour after Mr. Green's call to her. We were alerted by Washington that Ms. Osborne withdrew approximately five thousand dollars within a half hour of the call, and exchanged cars with her hairdresser."

"Her hairdresser?" The judge stared at the agent. "That's almost comical. Okay, go on."

"Yes, sir, it was her hairdresser's car. We found it in the parking lot of the Syracuse airport two days later. An airline check revealed she'd caught a United flight to Boston at midnight, and boarded another United flight to Chicago, which departed at two a.m., about a half-hour after she landed from Syracuse. We had agents at O'Hare within a half-hour of the arrival of the Boston flight, and determined she didn't book passage on any other flight. She could have taken a shuttle to the railroad station or bus terminal before we had agents there. She still could be in Chicago. That was our last contact."

Judge Devon sat back in his chair with his eyes shut. Several seconds passed before he began to speak.

"When you entered her home, did you examine the china closet, the one she referred to in the telephone call?"

"Not at that time, sir. But we sealed the house when we left and we returned the next day. At that time we examined the china closet."

"Were photographs taken of the inside of the house during the original search?"

"No, sir. We didn't believe it necessary or warranted at that time."

"All right, proceed."

Agent McGee put his notes down and continued his narrative. "Upon examination of the china closet we were able to discern a dust-free area. It was quite faint because of the glass doors. Nevertheless, the spot clearly indicated an object had recently stood there. We called in the forensic unit to measure and photograph the pattern. Would you like to see photographs of our findings?"

The judge leaned forward. "Yes."

Agent McGee produced several 8½" by 11" colored photographs from his notes and positioned them before the judge. "These photographs," he continued, "have been enhanced to clearly define the configuration of the pattern. As you can see, it is almost a perfect circle with a diameter of slightly greater than three inches. But notice the faint protuberance on the right side. I should add that photographs were taken facing the cabinet to represent the visual sides of the objects displayed."

"So," the judge stated, "whatever it was it had a round base with something sticking out, right?"

The agent smiled. "Well, not necessarily, your honor. That is one possible scenario. That pattern could also have been caused by what we call an umbrella configuration. The base could be any shape with a size smaller than three inches, but with some superstructure acting as a dust shield."

The judge absorbed that logic before posing his next question. "Did you examine the cabinet for any other objects that might have caused a similar pattern?"

"Judge," McGee responded with a tone of satisfaction, "you're getting ahead of me. Yes, sir, and on the shelf immediately below the one in question we found an object that cast this pattern." He indicated another photograph placed along side of the first. The patterns were virtually identical. The photo showed a ceramic coffee mug with a picture of a sandy beach and ocean waves crashing in the surf. In gold letters was OCEAN CITY MARYLAND.

"You see, Judge," Agent McGee continued, "the handle was the umbrella or shield causing the protuberance. The missing object is a mug."

Judge Devon examined the pictures for several seconds before responding, "And," prompting McGee to continue.

"We sent agents to Ocean City, and in fact to all the resorts on the Maryland, lower Delaware, and northern Virginia coasts. There was no sign of any fugitive."

Judge Devon picked up the photograph of the coffee mug and studied it. He muttered more to himself than to the others. "A coffee mug. She took a goddamn coffee mug. Jesus Christ, good thing she didn't dust too often." Then, turning to John King, he stated, "All right, who's next?"

Agent Fallon began. "Your honor, my report will be brief, I'm sad to say. We still haven't located Dr. Goldman. We have surveillance and taps on every known acquaintance. To the best of our knowledge she has no family and she has no known credit or bank accounts, at least in her name. There is a nationwide security alert for her. We'll find her."

"How long has it been, Agent Fallon, since the last known contact?" the judge said.

"She left the Virginia facility at Tyson's Corners approximately eight months ago after working on a Saturday. She logged out at five p.m. She wasn't reported missing until the following Monday when she didn't report for work. The local police were initially involved but found nothing. Her car was gone and many of her clothes. We later determined she'd withdrawn about fifty-thousand dollars in cash from her bank, and had cashed in another hundred and fifty thousand in bonds and securities."

"What about her records at work?"

"There were no records that we could find."

"That's it?"

"Yes, sir, that's it for now."

Judge Devon stood up. "Thank you all for a comprehensive briefing. Would you please excuse Mr. King and me?"

John King nodded to the agents. They packed their documents and left the room. When they were gone,

Judge Devon moved to the chair next to King and turned it so he faced Mr. King.

"They were amateurs, Mr. King, and you let them get away." He spoke in a low, methodical voice, the tone he had used as a trial lawyer in summations.

"No, your honor, that's not quite right." A hint of anger reflected in Mr. King's voice. "We had no reason to anticipate anything like that phone call and their responses."

Judge Devon didn't change his controlled manner. "You could've had them under direct surveillance, couldn't you?"

"Of course, we could have." John King's voice rose and his words were hurried. "And," he continued, "we could've had agents at their banks and at the airports. But there was no indication of the necessity for such operations. Remember, after the interrogation here, we had no reason to believe they were withholding information. I don't believe we acted improperly, given the circumstances. We'll find them. That I assure you."

The judge glared. "Listen to me carefully. I want to tell you some things you should know." King returned the stare for a moment and then averted his eyes from the judge's gaze. He didn't respond.

"Do you know what is my greatest pleasure as a judge? Now that, of course, is a rhetorical question. When lawyers appear before us to argue a case generally, but not always, they're very good. They don't get before the United States Supreme Court unless they're good. One measure of their capability is their preparedness. Before I was a judge, I argued cases before appellate courts, including the Supreme Court. I was one of the very good ones, Mr. King, and I'll tell you my secret. I had this overwhelming fear of being caught unprepared for some question a judge might ask. Now fear, Mr. King, is a great motivator and my fear bordered on the irrational. That was the key to my success. I researched everything, thought of every possibility, no matter how remote. But there was always one judge, damn him, who would pose the ultimate question from nowhere. Think of it. You're standing there intellectually naked before an audience awaiting an immediate response to an unanswerable question. I'll tell you how I dealt with it. You can't stand there longer than five seconds without talking. Then you start while the brain is computing. There's an answer, a response…find it, frame it, bring it into focus. Correlate with the facts, the law. Respond clearly, cogently in real time. I did that. If I couldn't do that I would've failed and I wouldn't be where I am today. It took intellect, knowledge, and most of all, fear of failure. So, what is my greatest pleasure today? I'm that judge, that sonofabitch judge who asks the questions from nowhere. I watch the attorney and measure his caliber as I count the seconds of silence before his response. This tells me about his character, how much he wants to succeed and more critically, how much he fears failure. Now, Mr. King, I want to see how you respond."

King twisted in his chair and then stood up. "Judge Devon, I understand what you want and what you have a right to expect." He paused, seeming to wait for some acknowledgment, but the judge didn't speak.

"I am a professional. I've been with the FBI for over twenty-five years and know what is expected of me and my staff. We won't disappoint you."

Judge Devon rose and looked at his watch. "I must leave," he said, "but I want you to understand what I'm going to say. First, you have a commitment of unlimited resources at your disposal. Whatever is required you either presently have or can have by asking me. Do you require anything to expedite this operation? People, money, facilities?"

"No, we have everything we need. I will keep you informed if that changes." King sighed.

"Very well. Here is the second point. We are running out of time. There is a limited and dwindling supply of serum. When it is depleted, it won't matter if you find them or not. It'll be too late for us. So be advised, Mr. King, that I have reallocated your allowance. As the supply diminishes the allocations are adjusted toward the top. We have passed your level, sir. So, if you don't want to wake up some morning soon, when the sun is shining on a bright world, and find Dorian Gray staring at you from your mirror, find those people. Good-night."

CHAPTER TEN

Despite the accident, Rachel Devon felt herself a very lucky young woman. She lived with her father in a lovely, colonial-style brick home in northwest Washington, D. C., and was an honor student, a senior at Georgetown University Law School. She knew that her father, being a justice of the United States Supreme Court, didn't impair her opportunities. She also knew that the law firms and corporations already wooing her wouldn't be doing so if she weren't in the top 5% of her class and co-editor of the law review. She took justifiable pride in her accomplishments.

There were the times, to be expected, when Rachel missed her mother and wished she could be her friend and confidant again. Perhaps, because she was an only child, she felt the emptiness so much. But Rachel was, by nature, an upbeat person, like her mother. After the accident that took her mother's life and left Rachel confined to a wheelchair, she adjusted, with pain to be sure, but also with spirit. Her mother would have understood, she knew. Her father, however, was a different breed. She loved him and realized how very much he loved her, but the judge had never healed from the loss of his wife. His wounds remained forever open and raw but concealed from the world. He lived a very inner life. Rachel felt it her duty to bring him happiness — bring light and music into his life, ease his contemplative morbidity, so she tried to provide a busy environment. She scheduled concerts, plays, dinner with friends, and vacations, attempting to intrude some happiness into what might have been his perpetual world of anger and mourning. She sheltered him from her dark moments, the times she cried alone on her pillow at night, wondering how she could ever know the love of a man. Don't speak of a just God to the judge, however. God never became rehabilitated from the iniquity of depriving Rachel's mother of her life and happiness.

Mrs. Martin, the housekeeper, must have heard the front door open. "Judge, how good to see you home in time for dinner." She took his coat and hung it in the closet. "Rachel will be delighted. I'll tell her you're here."

He smiled at her. "If she is studying don't bother her. I'll see her at dinner. I'll go in the library and watch TV."

"Scotch on the rocks to ease the news?" She chuckled.

"Sounds like a plan, Katherine. Thanks. What's for dinner tonight?"

"How about pot roast, mashed potatoes, and key lime pie for dessert?"

"You sure know the way to a man's heart, don't you?" They both laughed. He went into the library where he settled into his red leather recliner and switched on the TV. Before he could adjust to the CNN channel, he heard the familiar sound of his daughter's wheelchair coming down the corridor.

"I thought I heard you come in."

He loved the way she smiled at him. "Come over here. Let me hug you."

She held his glass of scotch in her hand and gave it to him as he bent down, brushed her dark bangs aside and kissed her on the forehead. Her right arm reached up, encircled his neck drawing his head down where she kissed him three times on the cheek.

He breathed deeply. It was good to be home.

Leaning back in his recliner, he drank from his glass as his daughter turned toward him.

"So, Pops, how was your day today? Reverse any states? Engage in any judicial activism?"

With a grin, he reached over to touch her face. "No more than the usual. And how about you, young lady? What esoteric jurisprudential principles did you probe today?"

"Bingo," she said. "You don't know how on target you are. We had a heated discussion about the World War II Japanese internment cases. Most of the class believed the cases were wrong, legally and morally, and could never recur. Dr. James seemed to agree, but, in all honesty, he just let us go at it. What's your opinion?"

Her father assumed his judicial demeanor.

"Well now, counselor, before the court renders its opinion, shouldn't we hear from counsel first? Proceed with your analysis. Convince us of your opinion."

"Why did I know you'd say that?" She loved to tease her dad. "Seriously, I'm conflicted. I know that it's easy to criticize in retrospect. We know that the decisions were based on false information and erroneous assumptions, that they blatantly violated the most solemn parts of the constitution. But I have that feeling of doubt, deep down, that if I had to make the judgment, at that time, with what I knew then, would I have had the courage to do differently? And would it have been right? I don't know. So, now your turn. Enlighten me and I promise I won't quote you in class."

"You damn well better not." He frowned. "But your doubts are well taken. I'll tell you what these cases mean. When the country is threatened, and by that I mean that the very institutions of state are threatened with destruction, the first rule is survival. Forget the judicial system, the rule of law, the constitution. If there is no state there is no rule of law. So we collectively crawl out of our cloak of civility and become lawless savages, if this is what it takes to survive. It's the supreme law of man, and all living things, individually and collectively — survival, the first Darwinian principle. That's what happened during the Civil War when Lincoln unilaterally suspended the Writ of

Habeas Corpus and defied the direct order of Chief Justice Taney. That's what happened at the onset of World War Two."

"But, Dad," she argued, "we apologized to the internees. We admitted that it was wrong. We paid reparations. Doesn't that mean we recognized the illogic and immorality of those cases?"

"We always revert to civility when the threat is over. That's the wonder of our system, our society."

He gave a sweeping gesture to the shelves of law books lining the walls.

"Read the Milligan case, which occurred after the Civil War. We return to the rule of law as soon as possible, put the beast back in the cave, and atone for the necessity of letting it out. But, and this is the crux of the matter, individually, or collectively, if what we hold dear is threatened again, we'll do whatever is deemed necessary at the time, to defend it."

Rachel paused to ponder that for several seconds before replying. "I understand. I suppose we can only hope that we're never faced with such a situation again. But if we are, I'm glad that my pop will be making the decisions."

He finished his drink, reached over and squeezed her hand as the obsessive thoughts again recurred. Someday we'll find the cure. Time won't run out, I promise. And I will walk proudly down the aisle with my tall, lovely daughter walking beside me. I will dance with her at her wedding and she will give me beautiful grandchildren. That's the least I can do for her mother. Survival, supreme law of nations, and man.

"Dinner, anyone?" Mrs. Martin stood in the doorway.

"Race you to the table, Pops." Rachel went scooting out of the room.

CHAPTER ELEVEN

Sheila Osborne stepped from the taxi at the front entrance of the Disneyland Resort Hotel in Anaheim, California. The breeze was warm against her face as the driver unloaded her one suitcase and delivered it to the doorman. It occurred to her there were no clothes in that suitcase appropriate for that climate. Albany was gray skies and cold rain that time of year. The past four days had been an adventure, a whirlwind of changing flights, running to taxis, and taking trains, a certain exhilaration in eluding the FBI agents whom she was certain were tracking her. She'd moved too fast and became too tired to feel apprehensive until now. David didn't know when she would arrive. They hadn't set a place to meet, only the location where the picture of her and her father was taken. But Disneyland is a gigantic theme park with thousands of people. The thought occurred to her that she and David could pass each other many times and never meet. She paid the driver, tipped the doorman and approached a line of people in front of the registration desk. With faint hope of finding David, she surveyed the lobby.

The man in the gray suit and blue tie in the corner, he had the look of a cop. Is he watching me or just waiting for someone?

Sheila drew in a breath and held it for a several seconds before exhaling.

Calm down, girl. Stop acting like a scared rabbit.

The reception clerk smiled at her.

"I need a room. A single please." She smiled back.

"Do you have a reservation?"

"I'm sorry, no."

The smile vanished from the clerk's face. "Oh, dear," he said. "That's a problem. We're completely booked."

Sheila hesitated for a second. "Can you put me on standby in case someone fails to show up?"

The clerk seemed concerned. "If you aren't particular about what kind of room you get, then there's always the possibility of a cancellation or no-show. I can also call the other hotels nearby and try and get you in there."

"I'll wait for a while to see about a room here. This is really my preference."

"Why not wait in the lounge? I'll page you if something becomes available. Your name, please?"

"Sheila," she said without thinking. "Sheila Smith."

Oh, shit. Why did I do that?

"And how long will you be staying?" He had written the name on a pad and stood poised, pen in hand, waiting to continue.

"Oh, two maybe three days. I'm not quite sure."

"I've got that down and I'll do the best I can."

She felt her face flush as she turned away. I'm one helluva spy. I need a drink.

As she walked across the lobby toward the lounge, suitcase in hand, she smiled. Bet I'm the only person wearing a coat in Southern California.

David realized he would arrive at Disneyland before Sheila. He had no idea, though, how long it would take her to cross the country. If she was taking trains and buses it could be several days. He hoped she was clever enough to switch often. Also he realized they had not established a specific meeting place, but he reasoned they would meet at a hotel, as they needed rooms. Since the Disneyland Hotel seemed the logical choice, he registered there under a pseudonym and planned to spend his days in the park so as not to attract undue attention in the lobby. In the evenings he'd do the rounds of the hotels hunting for Sheila.

Alone, he wandered through throngs of parents, children, and groups of teenagers, laughing their way through the magical colors, sounds, and excitement. He pictured the bright, smiling face of the little girl in the snapshot holding tight to her father's hand. What wonderment it must have been for her, the strange buildings, the scary rides. What kind of a father would willingly leave that little girl? It was difficult, no, really impossible for him to reconcile the image of her father with that of his brother-in-law. All of a sudden, he realized the image of his sister was receding along with the sharp pain of her loss. As he thought of this, he reached for his left knee. The pain recurred like a conscience prick and he could see her running ahead on

the Inspiration trail, head turned, laughing at him —
"Catch me if you can."

He worked to control himself from checking his
watch and wishing the hours away. He was
apprehensive, and yes, frightened. He admitted he was
scared of those people who were hunting him like some
wild prey.

I haven't broken any law. Why should I be a
victim? I can see myself being surrounded by men in
trench coats hustling me away, chains biting into my
flesh, to some dark, rotting place where John King
would loom over me like an avenging apparition. "I
warned you, Mr. Green. You can't deny me, now. It's
too late."

He wished Sheila would arrive soon.

David walked into the lobby of the Disneyland
Resort Hotel at six o'clock of the third day since his
arrival. He tried to be casual as he scanned the people.

Was anyone watching him? What would an FBI agent look like?

He couldn't stop himself, although he realized he probably would never be able to spot one. Satisfied that Sheila wasn't in the lobby, he tried the lounge and there she was, sitting alone by a small table reading a book. His apprehension faded as he walked toward her. She looked up and smiled at his approach.

Those pale violet eyes. I almost forgot how beautiful they were.

She started to get up but he motioned her to stay.

"What can I say except I'm glad you're here."

In answer, she put her arms around him. He liked the feel of her body against his and the scent of her hair.

"David, sit down and let's catch our breath. God, it's good to see you."

He signaled for the waitress. "What are you having, Sheila?"

"The house chardonnay."

"I'll have Jack Daniels on the rocks." He reached across the table and took Sheila's hand.

"Tell me how you got here? What did you do?"

"That's a long story. I get tired just thinking about it, but I guess we do what we have to. I did what you told me. A little luck helped. At any rate, I'm here and you're here and I have no idea what to do next. I don't even know where I'm going to sleep tonight. The only thing I'm sure of is that I'm glad to see you and I'm hungry, so you can buy me a nice dinner tonight." She squeezed his hand

"Now," her eyes flashed violet specks, "aren't you curious to see it, you know Aunt Ruth's thing? I have it right beside my chair in my suitcase."

He became serious. "Not here? You're serious? You don't have a room?"

She explained that she was waiting for a cancellation.

He thought for a second, "Let's do this. We'll make reservations for dinner and then go to my room. You can leave your luggage there and we'll take a look at 'it.' By the way, what name did you give the reservation clerk?"

"Sheila Smith."

"Sheila Smith, huh? Real imaginative." He paused before continuing. "Sheila Smith meet David Smith. What a pair of spies we make. I guess that makes us related. C'mon cousin, let's make reservations, check out Auntie Ruth's thing and then have dinner."

His room, on the sixth floor, offered a panoramic view of the park to the west, as well as two queen-sized beds against the right wall and two armchairs set around a small table beneath the window. He placed her suitcase on the table and, as she neared it David noticed her glance around. Then she withdrew from her suitcase the item, wrapped in a small towel that had been cushioned between a sweater and a pair of slacks. She unwrapped the item, set it on the table, and closed the suitcase. After David lowered the suitcase to the floor, they sat down by the table and stared at the item in front of them — a coffee mug.

David regarded the mug for a moment, without touching it. "This is it?" As soon as he spoke the words, he realized he'd made a mistake.

"Yes," Anger flashed in her tone. "This is it. This is what I knocked myself out running across the country to bring to you."

"Okay. Don't get upset with me. I'm sorry. This can be very important. Let's take a good look at it."

Sheila bit her upper lip and sat back in her chair. David picked up the mug.

"Aunt Ruth gave it to you?"

"Yes. I thought I made that clear. She gave it to me as a gift during one of her visits. I drank my cocoa from it. I loved the bird on it. I thought it was a turkey."

The white mug displayed a large red bird in flight on the front. Beneath the bird were the words:

Golden Gate
RAPTOR
Observatory

On the back of the mug was the inscription:

19 Species of Birds of Prey
20,000 Raptors Annually
250 Volunteers
10 Years of Banding
Hawkwatching and Telemetry
GGRO'S FIRST DECADE

"Did Aunt Ruth tell you where she got this?"

"I honestly don't recall." Sheila's anger diminished. "I wish I could remember more. She might have said something, given a clue, but I don't remember."

The mug clinked against the table as he set it down. He reached over and took her hand in his.

"Hey." He smiled, "This is a start. She obviously had some connection with the Golden Gate Raptor Observatory. We'll start from there. Golden Gate indicates that this observatory, or whatever it is, must be in the Bay Area. I'm sure they have a San Francisco phone book in the hotel or we can call information."

"I don't think we should call information. Couldn't that be traced?"

"You're thinking," he said, "and I wasn't. Of course you're right. When we go down for dinner we'll check out the phone book. Would you like to freshen up before dinner?"

"You read my mind." She smiled, as she picked up her suitcase and headed for the bathroom.

They had a secluded table in Granville's Steak House Restaurant. The waiter lit a candle at the table.

David ordered a bottle of merlot to go with the steaks they selected.

"Strike two," David said. "Nothing in the San Francisco phone book, and no room for you, so far. At least we won't starve."

"What do you think we should do?" She swirled the wine in her glass.

"I'm not completely sure. The name Golden Gate certainly indicates San Francisco. There isn't any point in staying in Anaheim. The longer we're here the more chance someone will spot us. I think we should pack up tomorrow and head north."

"What do we do when we get to San Francisco?"

"I don't know. We'll have time to think about that on the ride up."

"Well," she smiled, "you were right when you said at least we wouldn't starve. Here come the steaks."

After dinner, the waiter cleared the table and brought them coffee. Soft music drifted into the dining room from the lounge — "Blue Moon, you saw me standing alone."

David spoke. "I really know very little about you."

Sheila sank back in her chair and fingered her coffee cup. "I guess there isn't much to tell. What you see is what you get. You know that my dad left when I was a kid. I really was close to my mother. She was such a good person. She always seemed to understand and be there when I needed her. She knew it even when I was a snotty kid. You don't know how miserable teenage girls can be." She paused and drank from her cup. "I loved her very much and I miss her. After high school, I went to Russell Sage College and got my BA in literature. I had aspirations of becoming a writer. We didn't have much money and I certainly couldn't support myself by writing so I went to school and became a physical therapist. I enjoy the work and it pays pretty well. After Mom died, three years ago, I kept the house on South Main and the rest you know."

"Well," hesitating, "not exactly."

She looked up at him. "What have I left out?"

"Doesn't it trouble you? Isn't there something wrong here, your father, my brother-in-law, the same person."

The waiter appeared and refilled the coffee cups.

"It does trouble me, deeply. I have no explanation."

He placed his hand on hers and smiled, "It's okay. We'll get some answers. On another subject, tell me how it was you left Albany when you did? I'm glad you did, just curious. What prompted you?"

She relaxed in her chair and touched a finger to her lip. "Perhaps my answer is too simple. Just how long could I sit on the porch rocker and watch the leaves blow down the street? My life needed change and I determined that a good start would be finding my father. I had nothing to lose."

"What about your job?"

"I gave them two weeks notice and quit. I can always get a job."

"No big love interests? No boy friend?"

"Not at the moment." She chuckled. "Oh, there have been boys, but no big crushes since high school. How about you?"

"None at the moment, either." He took a deep breath. "But I'm always ready to remedy that situation should the opportunity arise." He paused. "Sheila, why don't you stay in my room tonight? You saw there're two beds and it doesn't seem likely you'll get a room. That way we can get an early start tomorrow morning."

"Makes sense." She nodded. "Why not? You don't come across like Attila the Hun, so I guess I can trust you. Besides, look at the money I'll save." They giggled as they left the restaurant.

David turned off the nightlight leaving the room lit only by faint moonlight that filtered through the window where the drapes hadn't completely closed. He heard Sheila walk from the bathroom, pull the covers back and slip into her bed. He was somewhat aware of the scent of perfume.

"Goodnight, David." Her voice was soft.

"Goodnight, Sheila. I'm glad you're here."

"I know."

He turned on his side, doubled the pillow under his head and stared toward the window.

Here I am in Los Angeles, or somewhere, with this strange woman sleeping in the next bed. We have a coffee mug from some bird organization and the whole federal government looking for us. Everything began with the death of my poor sister, my big sister, my best friend.

Once more he was back on the Inspiration Point Trail with Lee, running with the wind as he drifted to sleep.

David heard a sound, opened his eyes and tried to fathom its source. Earlier moonlight through the window had vanished and he couldn't see anything. Turning on his back he lay still.

"David," Sheila whispered.

He first sensed her standing over him and then could distinguish her silhouette in the dim light. She reached down, lifted his blanket and slid in beside him and whispered his name again, "I don't want to be alone tonight. Please, just hold me."

His arm encircled her shoulder and he pulled her next to him, her head resting on his shoulder. He touched her hair and stroked it back against the pillow. Then bending down, he brushed back her bangs with his hand, and kissed her on the forehead. Her breath warmed his neck and she turned toward him so that her body rested against his. Then she tilted her head, placed her hand behind his head and brought it down to her mouth. Her lips were full against his. He could sense flashes of violet fire from her eyes.

Alan J. Gould

CHAPTER TWELVE

Maureen Fallon straightened her coat and brushed her hair back with her right hand before reaching the door of The Prime Rib. As one of several restaurants and private clubs on K Street that hosted distinct cliques at noon and after work, The Prime Rib had its "in" crowd that collected in the lounge after work. John King liked being greeted by name by the bartender. He was considered a "regular" by the other "regulars." The Prime Rib was upbeat, attracting the management echelons of business and government, the gray suit, white shirt crowd. Agent Fallon and John King met there often after work. She never understood why he singled her out as an after-work friend, but she enjoyed the special relationship.

When Maureen spotted him sitting at a small table in the lounge, John King rose and beckoned to her. "Hi, there," he said. "Glad to see you. Give me your coat and I'll check it."

She smiled. "No thanks, John, I'll just slip it over my chair. How are you?"

"I guess saying that things could be better would be sort of an understatement. But let's have a drink and I'll fill you in." He ordered two Stoly martinis and leaned forward in his chair.

"He's a clever son-of-a-bitch, that David Green. You know what he did? He bought a used car out of the newspaper and paid cash for it. That means, of course, that wherever he was going he drove, and we have sent the alert with plate number and description. He's meeting her someplace and we'll find them."

Maureen Fallon didn't speak. Of course the obvious question was why these two seemingly innocuous people warranted the attention of a special operation and a Supreme Court Justice. She figured he'd fill in details when ready.

The drinks arrived. They clicked glasses, exchanged smiles, and then he hesitated for a moment before putting his hand over hers.

"What did you think of Judge Devon?"

Aha, he's getting down to it. "I thought he was very, how can I put it, judicial. How's that for an answer?"

With a laugh, John withdrew his hand and sat back in his chair. "Well," he replied, "your diplomacy is sparkling. It actually wasn't a very fair question, I guess, but it was perhaps an awkward way of involving you in more of the details of this operation. Are you interested?"

Maureen Fallon looked at John King. He must be about ten years or so older than me. I wonder if he was ever married. "Of course I'm interested. I'll do anything I can to help."

"Good," he answered. "I have a great idea. Briefing you is going to take some time, so let's have dinner. I understand that their prime rib is great. Will this work for you?"

"Well, let me think." She put her finger to her closed lips, "No, I don't think I have anything very special scheduled for the next few hours." Then she smiled. "Thanks, John, I'd love to have dinner with you."

Well, let's just put this in some perspective. I'm all of about five feet, six inches, not a great figure to be sure, but not too bad with the right clothes. Sure, face is sort of plain. Why didn't I do a little something with the make-up? But nice smile. Gotta get rid of the bun, though, at least after hours. I'll find a hairdresser. When was the last time someone asked me to dinner?

"John, why are you telling me all this? Why are you confiding in me?"

He had told her the full story, everything he knew, about Dr. Goldman, the serum, and the organization committed to obtaining it. Without hesitation he revealed his personal interest.

"Why me and not Carson or McGee?" Maureen said.

"I've been with the bureau for eighteen years. I've no complaints about the way I've been treated. Believe me, I think I deserve the trust, but it's always nice to know that you're appreciated. I didn't ask for this assignment. I didn't ask to be included as, I'm struggling for a word, let's say, a beneficiary. But once they waved that magic wand in front of me, I became as obsessed as the others. I'd go back to my apartment at night, pour a little scotch on the rocks, dim the lights, listen to some classical music station, and daydream about how I would spend the next three or four hundred years. It was exhilarating, exciting...I could feel my heart beat when I thought about it. Just the concept was sufficient, the freedom it created, to take time, all the time, to do whatever I wanted. Can you understand that?"

Unsure what to say, Maureen was glad when the waiter came to clear the table. Then she confronted him. "Why me, John?"

"I thought we were friends. More than just business associates, and we could confide in each other. Does that make sense?"

"Not really," she said without a smile, "but proceed."

"Well, I got angry, very angry. I didn't need to be bribed to do my job. I felt like a whore because I didn't turn them down immediately. And I began thinking about that three or four hundred gifted years...what the hell would I do with them? If anything, I try to be honest with myself, and I don't think that in another three hundred years I could be anything more than I am now. So what's the point?"

"So what are you going to do?" she said.

"Well, first, I'm going to have a cup of coffee, good, rich, leaded coffee, and eat some obscenely fattening dessert, and I hope you'll join me. "

"Good." She smiled. "Sounds really good."

"Then tomorrow," he said, "I'll start planning what I'll do when I get my hands on that David Green. The more I think about it, the more I believe I could kill him."

She squinted at him perplexed. "You would kill Mr. Green?"

"No," he answered, "Judge Devon."

They both laughed. Maureen wondered where they were going with that.

Alan J. Gould

CHAPTER THIRTEEN

"K inko's," he announced. Sheila put down her cup of coffee and smiled.

"There's a Kinko's on West Katella Avenue which is almost around the corner from us. I'll bet the Golden Gate Raptor Observatory has a web site. I don't know if you have Kinko's in Albany, but you can rent computer time from them. We'll go and check 'em out."

"Okay, we'll check out the Raptor thing and then what?"

"We'll see if we can find Aunt Ruth. I think that's the plan, and I also believe we should get out of Southern California as fast as possible. I don't want to underestimate them, Sheila. I assume they know about my car by now. We don't have much of a choice except to keep it, but we can be smart and careful, and that means we must keep moving. So let's check out of here quickly, quietly, and on to Kinko's."

The Golden Gate Raptor Observatory

Every autumn thousands of migrating birds of prey appear over the Golden Gate near San Francisco, California.

Why are they here? How are they doing?"

Where do they go?

That's just what we're here to learn.

The Golden Gate Raptor Observatory (GGRO) has three staff members and more than 250 community volunteers, all dedicated to studying the autumn hawk migration. The GGRO's guiding philosophy is that public involvement is a critical, yet often ignored component of long-term wildlife conservation.

The GGRO's mission is to inspire the preservation of California raptor populations. The GGRO was formed in the early 1980s to track the Golden Gate migration, an annual flight of thousands of hawks, eagles, falcon, and vultures — birds collectively called raptors.

The office is at Building Ten, Fort Cronkite near the field of operations at "Hawk Hill," overlooking San Francisco Bay from the Marin Headlands.

David copied the information down on a pad, closed the computer, paid for the computer rental, and then joined Sheila who'd waited for him in the car he'd parked on the side of a building away from the main road.

"What did you find, for God's sake. Tell me. I can't stand it."

"It was all there. Just what we wanted to know. We're on our way to San Francisco. Have you ever been there?"

"No," she answered. "Tell me about it."

"You'll love it." He smiled and draped his arm around her. "Have you ever had cioppino or Dungeness crab? Of course not. Well, you'll see the world's prettiest city and, with a little bit of luck, we may even locate dear Aunt Ruth counting her birds. First, though, how would you like to go to a movie?"

"Are you nuts?" She pulled away and glared at him.

"Do you know you have violet eyes and sometimes they really sparkle, like right now. " He lifted her chin and kissed her. "Yes," he said, "I'm probably nuts. I admit it. But we'll park this car, the only one we have or can get, in a garage. No one will find it there. We'll kill some time until the afternoon commute and then head north. When we're out of the commute jam, we'll stop somewhere and eat dinner, kill some more time until its gets dark. Then we'll drive on to the Bay Area. I think that's the best way to avoid being discovered."

"We're on our way to Los Angeles." John King motioned agents Carson, McGee, and Fallon to take their seats in the briefing room.

"The car was ID'd and the two of them identified at the Disneyland Hotel. Los Angeles, San Francisco, and San Diego have been alerted, as well as the local police and the Highway Patrol. We're out of here in an hour."

At five o'clock, Sheila and David exited onto Interstate 5 and headed north. As anticipated, the commute traffic was quite congested.

"We'll hang in this traffic as long as it lasts," he said.

"Aren't we more at risk stopping where the car can easily be spotted rather than continuing?"

"You may be right. Let's think about it." David smiled at her before returning his attention to the road. "I don't know where we're going with this, but I do know one good thing came out of this, meeting you."

He put his arm around her as she put her head on his shoulder. They continued in silence for a while before David spoke. "I was wondering about Aunt Ruth. She seems to be the critical element in this whole thing. How well did you know her? What can you tell me about her?"

Sheila didn't move from his shoulder. Several seconds later, she answered, "I'll tell you her early background." She paused, again, before continuing. "We were sitting in the living room in the house on South Main Street. My mother, in the large rocker, was crocheting a shawl and I sat on the sofa next to Aunt Ruth with my head on her shoulder. I suppose that's why I remember it so clearly." She pressed her head into his shoulder and he squeezed her.

"It must have been the time she brought me the mug because I was holding it on my lap. I don't know what I was thinking but I said something like 'Aunt Ruth, do you have parents or children?' She ran her fingers through my hair. 'No, sweetheart,' she said. 'I don't have my parents and I never had any children because I never was married.' I thought about that and said, 'But you did have a mommy and daddy, didn't you?' When she didn't answer me, I looked up at her and saw that she was looking at my mother. Mom didn't say anything but nodded her head. Aunt Ruth turned to me and said, 'You want to hear about my family, sweetheart? All right, I'll tell you'."

CHAPTER FOURTEEN

I was about your age, and lived with my mother and father in a great house in a city in Germany. I had a younger brother who I loved even though he was a pest at times. My dad was a clockmaker and had his shop on the first floor. It was a wonderful place, always filled with the sounds of clocks ticking, cuckoos popping in and out, and little carved figures parading around. He'd perch on a tall stool over his workbench, and I'd drag over another stool so I could sit beside him and watch him work. I knew better than to disturb him. He smoked a big, old yellow pipe and I loved the smell of the smoke as it curled around me. His hands were large and his fingers short and pudgy. I remember wondering how those pudgy fingers could handle the tiny tools he used to fix his clocks.

Every so often, he'd smile at me and pat me on the head. I think he liked having me there. He wasn't a tall man, but he had big shoulders and arms. Sometimes he'd pick me up so I could see the clocks on the shelves or those hanging on chains from hooks in the ceiling. I loved to touch them and he never told me not to, or to be careful. I remember that so well and I was careful. My mother was a big woman. She always seemed to be wearing an apron and cooking in the kitchen or reading books to my brother and me. She would gather us, place one on either side of her and open a book.

"A book is a precious thing," she would say. "You learn from books and that is the way knowledge gets passed from one person to another. Never forget, books contain the thoughts and feelings of a person. That means you must always treat the book as you would the person, with care and respect."

She always told my brother and me about the author before reading to us. And could my mother cook. What a wonderful cook, but her specialty was baking. She would bake beautiful pastries and breads, and she always made little loaves for my brother and me.

I attended a school about five blocks from our house. A boy who lived across the street also went to the same school. We were friends and would walk together. He was a little older than me, and I think he liked me. Sometimes he'd hold my hand and carry my books. His name was Hans, Hans Holtz. I liked to say his name because it sounded sort of musical. One day, I started to school and Hans wasn't there. That wasn't too unusual and I didn't think much about it. When I arrived at school, one of the teachers stood in front of the entrance blocking me.

"Go home," he said. "You can't come here, anymore."

I didn't know what to do or say. I stared up at him and I remember the look on his face.

"Get out of here now and go home. You can't come here anymore," he repeated, arms folded across his chest. When he said that he half smiled. I couldn't understand why he smiled when he told me I couldn't go to school. Some of the children gathered around and a boy shoved me on the shoulder.

"Get out of here," he shouted, using a bad word. Someone else kicked me in the legs and I fell down. My books scattered on the ground. I tried to reach for them but someone kicked them away. I scrambled home. My father picked me up in his arms, kissed me, and wiped the tears and blood from my cheeks. He closed and locked the door to the shop and carried me upstairs.

My parents spoke in soft voices. I didn't know what they were saying and I was frightened.

My father put both his hands on either side of my face and gently lifted my head so I was staring straight into his eyes.

"Listen to me, Rutie," he said. "Listen very carefully. From now on your mother and I will teach you at home. You won't go back to the school. And there is something else." My mother handed him my dress coat, the blue one with the shiny patent leather belt and silver buckle that I would wear on special occasions.

"I'm pinning this envelope inside your coat. It's important. You're to keep this coat near you when you go to bed tonight, and every night. Remember this carefully. If your mother or I should call you, and we might do this in a whisper, you understand? You will go to the big closet in the hall. Come with me. I'll show you."

Clutching my hand, he showed me the closet, which was very deep and lined with cedar. A chest stood on the right side and the rest of the closet had shelves with folded linens, china that was used for holidays, and various other occasions.

"You're to climb behind the big chest where you'll find a blanket. Cover yourself with the blanket and don't make a sound. Understand? Not one sound. Wait until we come for you. If we don't come, stay there until someone like Aunt Jenny comes. Keep your coat with you. Don't be scared and always be very quiet no matter what you hear. Do you understand?"

I was scared and didn't understand at all. My face hurt where I'd hit the ground.

I never returned to school. Every day my mother read to my brother and me, and told us stories. One evening, my mother and father sat down with us and told us that we would be leaving that night. They didn't say where we would be going, only that we would be carrying very few things and we should be very quiet. I thought about all of the clocks in the shop below and wondered if we would be taking them. I was packing my small bag in my room when I heard a sharp crashing sound. It came from downstairs, near the front door. Men were yelling, but I couldn't understand what they were saying. Suddenly I felt my father's hand on my shoulder. I turned and saw his finger over his mouth.

"Shhh, come with me, quickly." He whispered. "Remember what I told you. Take your coat, the blue one."

I picked it up and he walked me to the closet where my mother stood. I heard another loud sound from downstairs, and shouts. She picked me up and pressed her face next to mine. I could feel her tears run down my cheek.

"Rutie, my baby, I love you, love you. Now, go in there and be quiet, very quiet, no matter what. Stay there."

I covered myself with the blanket behind the large chest. I heard sounds, coughing, voices, but I couldn't understand what was being said. Every so often I heard a crash and sometimes the sound of glass breaking. I moved the blanket a little bit away from my face so I could breathe and I stretched my legs, slowly, one at a time, so as not to make any noise. The door of the closet suddenly opened. I tried to hold my breath and not move, but I felt my feet scraping along the floor and sweat drip into my eyes. I curled down deep inside the blanket choking back the tears. The chest lid opened and I could hear the creak of its hinges. I lifted the blanket a little from my head and slid it down just so I could peer over the edge. The light was very bright and I could see someone silhouetted in the closet entrance. It was a man, but I couldn't see his face. He wore a cap and hair protruded out in tufts like pine needles. He looked around and suddenly, with one wave of his arm, swept the china from the shelf to the floor where it shattered and spilled across the floor. One broken teacup stopped at the foot of my blanket as I pulled my head down and shivered.

Everything grew still. I didn't move. I wanted to cry but knew I shouldn't. That was a terrible thing, when you want to cry, need to cry, and can't. It didn't matter whether I kept my eyes open or shut because it was all darkness and I wondered how I would know when it was light and if someone would come for me. I waited, but no one came.

What would I do if I had to go to the bathroom?

I realized I had wet myself. I didn't know when it happened. I don't know how long I stayed under the blanket, but finally I pushed it down from my head again, so I could peer out. The closet door was a little ajar and I could see light and knew it was daytime. Carefully, I left my refuge and tiptoed to the closet door. I touched it, gently. It opened onto overturned furniture and broken glass. Everything was quiet. I really didn't know what to do. I went from room to room but no one was there. I started to walk down the stairs and remembered what my father had said, "Don't forget the blue coat." I went back to the closet, picked up the coat and carried it downstairs. I walked out into the street and at first the bright light of the sun hurt my eyes. I turned and looked at the front of my father's shop. The window was broken, shards slanted into the empty space. I saw his stool upended, broken clocks on the floor. How strange it seemed without the sounds of the cuckoos. The torn books, precious books, lay strewn amongst the clocks along with my father's yellow pipe, burnt tobacco spilling from the bowl.

I felt a hand tighten on my shoulder and tensed, sure that I was going to be thrown to the ground again.

"My God, Ruthie." It was Hans. We stared at each other for a minute. I didn't know what to do or say. He repeated himself, "Oh, my God, Ruthie," and then looked quickly in both directions. He grabbed my hand and pulled me. "Hurry, someone might see us."

He half pushed and dragged me across the street and up the steps into his house. "Mother," he yelled.

"Come quickly." His mother came into the room and whispered, "Oh, my God," picked me up and hugged me. That was the first time I felt I could cry. I buried my head in her chest and sobbed. She said nothing, holding me close and rocking back and forth. Hans closed the drapes over the windows fronting the street.

I stayed with the Holtz's for two days, sleeping in the guest room and staying away from the windows. When I think back to those two days, I wonder why I wasn't curious about my parents and my brother. Now I understand my feelings at that time, intellectually that is. However, I can't completely repress a sense of guilt. Of course I was in a state of shock, emotionally numb, but it was more than that. I intuitively knew that my family was gone. But I was glad I was alive. How do you live with that?

On the second day, when we gathered in the living room, Mr. Holtz took my hand. "It isn't safe for you to stay with us. We've made arrangements for you, and tonight Hans will take you away. We want you to be safe, Ruth, and this is the best thing."

I never asked them about my parents or my brother. I was afraid to see their faces if I did.

I left the Holtz' house that night with Hans. He led me through the half empty streets, holding my hand and staying close to the buildings, avoiding the lights.

I'd been in a church, of course. My parents never said anything to me about churches, but it seemed that we always walked a little faster when we passed one. I knew it was a church because of the cross over the entrance and the tall belfry. Every Sunday morning I liked hearing the songs of the bells.

Hans whispered, "Do exactly as I do." He squeezed my hand as we entered the church, lit by candles. My first sensation was the smell of melting wax. Next, I saw the giant crucifix over the altar and was transfixed by the image. Here was this man, this thin man, with his hands and feet nailed to a cross and his head bowed to the right, with the shimmering light from the candles seeming to give his form a life sense. Hans tugged my hand. I noticed there were some people in the pews, not many, but a few heads turned toward us.

"Just do as I do," he said. He paused at a large marble bowl on a pedestal near the entrance and dipped his hand in it. There was water in the bowl and Hans crossed himself. I did the same. He led me to a pew in the rear, away from the few people.

"Sit here. I'll be back soon."

I sat and waited for Hans to return, but I never saw him again.

A priest came from in back of the church and sat down next to me.

"I'm Father Alfred, your friend. Don't be frightened. Now listen to me, carefully. When I get up, you get up, also, just like I do. Then follow me and, don't forget your coat."

I had never been close to a priest, much less spoken to one. I had no idea who this person was or what he wanted from me, but I followed him into a small room in the back of the church.

"Sit down," he said, "and rest. Are you hungry? Would you like something to eat, drink?"

I nodded my head sideways and said, "Where is Hans?"

"Hans has left. Hans is a good friend and wants us to take good care of you." He knelt down so he could look in my eyes. "I know you have sorrow and I share that with you. But I promise, you'll be safe. Try and rest."

He left the room, turning and smiling at me as he shut the door. I closed my eyes, but couldn't sleep. The sounds of shattering glass and the images of torn books and broken clocks intruded into my thoughts, and as hard as I tried, I couldn't recall images of my mother and father. I wondered if my brother still hid in some closet in our house.

Despite everything, I did doze off because I can only recall someone shaking my shoulder with gentle hands. It seems there were always hands on my shoulder. When I opened my eyes, Father Alfred smiled at me.

"Come. Don't be afraid and don't forget your coat."

It was in the early light of dawn when the car turned into a driveway leading to a tall building silhouetted against the morning sky. A cross reached skyward from the roof. The car neared the building along the road lined with trees and flowering bushes that sparkled with the early morning dew. Chiseled in stone over the entrance, I read SANKT MARIA.

When the car stopped, a figure emerged from the shadows at the entrance. Of course I had seen nuns on the streets of our city. If they were approaching me on the sidewalk, I would cross the street or press against a wall to let them go by. Dressed in black, with their heads covered and their faces framed by starched white, they seemed as if from another world, a threatening world that I was not a part of. The nun opened the car door and studied me without expression. She extended one thin hand, grasped my coat and, with the other, beckoned to me. "Follow me," she said. I did, through several corridors and to a door that led into a small room with a bed in one corner and a chest of drawers in another. A silver pitcher and bowl sat on the dresser. Over the bed was a picture of the man nailed to a cross.

"Wait here," she said, "and I'll get you some things."

In a few minutes, she returned with towels, soap, a toothbrush, toothpaste, and a nightgown.

"Why don't you wash up and change, and I'll be back shortly."

Before I could say anything, she left, so I did as I was bid and then waited on the bed. Soon the door opened and she entered.

"Your name is Ruth, is that right?"

"Yes."

"I'm Mother Agnes and this is Saint Mary's orphanage for girls. I know you are frightened and have many questions. I promise you two things, Ruth. First, you are safe here with us, and second, all your questions will be answered in time. All we ask of you is to trust us. Now, I know you must be tired, so try to sleep and tomorrow you'll see everything."

Before I could say anything, she stood up, left the room and closed the door behind her.

I awoke to a knock on the door. My first thought was that this was strange. Mother Agnes didn't knock, she just entered. I opened the door and another nun was standing there, not as tall as Mother Agnes. She smiled when she spoke.

"I'm Sister Dorothy, and I'm to be your special friend while you are here with us. Get dressed and we'll go to the dining hall for breakfast."

I didn't realize how hungry I was and hurried to do as I was told. The dining hall had many long tables and benches. Girls were standing in the serving line and bringing their trays to a table. I noticed that the noise level wasn't anywhere as high as in the school cafeteria. The girls seemed about my age, some older, some younger, and all were dressed the same in plaid skirts and white shirts. Sister Dorothy and I went through the serving line and took our trays to the end of one of the tables where we were somewhat separated from the others.

"After breakfast we'll get you outfitted and then we'll talk a little. I'll answer your questions, as many as

I can, and tell you about Sankt Maria and what you will be doing here."

We were seated facing each other across a desk in an office. She grabbed my hand, smiled, and I sat back, a little less tense.

"You must do what all the girls here do, Ruth. That isn't the only rule, but it is the most important one. That means you will say the prayers in the classroom and go to mass with everyone. You will kneel and cross yourself. I'll show you how, and take the sacrament at the mass with the others. Again, I will show you. I want you to listen to what I have to say very carefully and try to understand. We know you aren't a Catholic. We aren't trying to make you become a Catholic. But we don't want anyone else to know that you're not a Catholic. Do you understand?'

I nodded that I understood even though I didn't. She seemed to sense that.

"I know you don't understand all the reasons for this, but I just want you to know one thing. Ruth, we love you and you must trust us. If you ever have doubts or questions or any problems, please come to me, not anyone else. Not to any friends you might make here, and you will, of course. Come only to me. Will you promise me that?"

I nodded and she smiled at me.

"Now let's get started. Let's see, what size skirt do you take?"

I spent the next two years at Sankt Maria. I roomed with three other girls my age and followed the daily routine of school, prayers, and study. At that orphanage I discovered my love of math and science with the encouragement of the teachers. I realized later that girls never had the opportunity to study those subjects in the regular schools but Sankt Maria was different. The nuns encouraged our development and I think they took delight in seeing us excel in subjects reserved for men.

We knew there was a war raging about us. We heard radio broadcasts at night and sometimes could hear planes flying overhead. Through opened windows, we could hear the moan of distant sirens, muffled explosions, and could see the arcs of anti-aircraft lights sweeping the skies. Sometimes there wasn't the usual food, and milk was scarce, but generally, the war didn't affect us until near the end. I remember watching the retreating columns of soldiers across the road silhouetted against the dusty sky. How young they seemed. Some wandered onto our campus and the nuns treated the wounded as best they could in the infirmary. Then it was quiet.

Sister Dorothy called me into the library and beckoned me to sit down at a table in the corner.

"The war is over." She hesitated. I sensed she didn't quite know how to continue, but I said nothing.

"You've become a beautiful young woman in the years you've been with us. What a sweet treasure you are."

Again she hesitated and I could see her eyes glisten. I put my arm around her.

"I love you, Sister." I didn't know what else to say.

She gently pushed me away, wiped her eyes and continued. "Tomorrow you will be leaving us."

I stood up. "Why? Where will I go? I don't want to leave. Please don't send me away."

"Sit down and listen to me, Ruth. Listen carefully. I want to explain everything to you. Tomorrow, a woman will come here, an American, from a Jewish organization that takes care of Jewish children, like you, who have lost their parents in the war. They want to help you so you must go with her and do what she says. These are your people. Promise me that you will go and do what they say."

The next morning, I packed my clothes, said goodbye to my friends. Sister Dorothy took my hand as we neared the front foyer. A woman stood there. She was tall and thin, and I remember thinking how pretty she looked. She extended her hand and said, "Hello, Ruth, I'm Rose. I've come to help and be your friend." She took my bag from Sister Dorothy who knelt and hugged me.

"Don't say anything," she whispered.

As I started to leave I heard a voice.

"Ruth, you forgot something."

I turned around and saw Mother Agnes standing there with my blue coat folded over her arm, the one with the patent leather belt and silver buckle.

"And remember the envelope pinned inside," she said.

CHAPTER FIFTEEN

The traffic remained heavy as they drove north. "See if you can get any news."

Sheila turned on the car radio and searched until she found a news station that reported the traffic conditions, the weather, and at 5:30, connected with the national network for world news. At 5:40, an announcer reported local news — a three vehicle accident with injuries on Route 118 north of Moorpark, expected delays due to fog on Route 210 north of San Fernando. At the conclusion of the detailed description of the Democratic primary race for mayor and interviews with the candidates, the announcer said, "Just in. A special police alert. The FBI has issued a special alert for a nineteen ninety-five Green Honda four-door Accord." He read the California license plate number and then said, "which is believed to be driven by David Green age thirty-four, traveling with Sheila Osborne, age twenty-eight. Both are wanted by the FBI on suspicion of stealing highly classified information. Anyone seeing them is asked to report immediately to the FBI or local police. The FBI warns that these people are considered dangerous and may be armed."

"Oh, my God!" Sheila screamed.

David didn't answer but his right foot hit the brake pedal. The car lurched. The driver behind them sounded his horn and veered to the right to avoid hitting our bumper. Recovering control, David turned on his right directional and when the right lane was clear, swerved into it and slowed. He reached into the rear pants pocket for his handkerchief and wiped sweat from his forehead and moisture from his lips.

"I've got to stop and think," he said.

"Where can we stop? What can we do? David, they'll kill us."

"We can't panic. That's what they want. Let's just drive slowly along and think."

They drove just below the speed limit in the right lane for several miles before he spoke. "Well, one thing's for sure. We can't continue on with this car."

"David, if they know about the car and they are broadcasting here, they must have found out that we were in Los Angeles."

"That's right. We have hard choices to make. I suppose we could continue north tonight. That is one choice. We'd have to stop for gas and that would be very dangerous. Another option is to ditch the car."

"If we dump the car we'll have to go by train or bus. Isn't that just as dangerous, if not more so?"

"Yes, that's true. But I still don't think we'll make it in this car all the way to San Francisco."

Sheila grabbed his arm. "Suppose we get another car. You know, the same way you got this one. We stop in the next town or somewhere, dump this one and buy another."

"Great idea but it won't work. They know about this car. That means they also are aware of how I got it in the first place. They'll be watching for us to do just that. They'll be checking the ads in all the papers around here and calling the people up to see if they sold their car."

"Look," she said. "Around Albany you always see cars parked with for sale signs on their windshields. They aren't advertised. Maybe we could find one of those. It would take them quite a while to track that down, wouldn't it?"

David's voice was low and deliberate. "I don't know what the hell we got ourselves into. All I wanted to discover was how my poor sister died and all you did was search for your father. Here we are, in Southern California with the whole world looking for us ready to kill us."

"What are you driving at?"

"Simply this. I'm not sure about you, but everything changed for me since that last night at the hotel. Yes, of course, I want to learn about Lee as much as you want to find your dad. And I don't like to be pushed around and treated like a criminal, especially by people like John King. But I'm wondering, what's really important? If you feel the same way about me as I feel about you, maybe, just maybe, we should pull into the next station and call John King. Give him the goddamn cup and let's get on with our lives, perhaps together. We need time, Sheila."

She sat without answering. The car continued at the speed limit in the right lane northward on Interstate 5.

"David, I truly have feelings for you. I don't have to tell you that. I want to have the time for us to know each other better and be able to, how can I express it, find each other in peace, without this horrible fear and stress. Really, believe me when I say this. But I feel something else. We started in this together with a purpose. Frankly, I'm not certain exactly what that was. I also want you to know that I'm scared, very scared. I'm not sure what we should do but one thing is for certain, we can't quit now. I want to see this through."

"Jesus, Sheila, we could be killed."

"I know."

David turned off Interstate 5 at the California 99 exit.

"We'll be in Bakersfield shortly. Maybe it'll still be light enough to find a car for sale. It won't be a very good or new car because we have to pay cash. Any large amount will raise suspicion."

It wasn't a car. It was a Chevy pickup truck, about ten years old, which they found in a gas station lot with a for sale sign and phone number.

David said, "I'll drive around the corner and get out. You stay with the car and I'll see about the truck."

He parked on a side street as far away as possible from the nearest street light, then called the number from the gas station and was lucky, because the owner was home and agreed to meet in fifteen minutes. David stood on the street side of the truck where he couldn't be seen from inside the station until the owner arrived. As he waited, two cars pulled into the station and he scanned them almost expecting to see men in dark coats leap out. The wind blew leaves down the street as David shivered, pulling his coat collar above his neck.

"Hi, there." A man extended his hand. As tall as David, in his mid-forties with tufts of black hair and strands of gray protruding from his cap, he said, "I'm Chuck Kinney and this is my truck. She's been driven some, as you can see, but she's sound, runs well. She'll need new brakes and tires soon but other than that she'll give good service."

David shook his hand. "I'm Bill Carpenter and that's what I'm looking for. Can I take her for a spin?"

"You've got it." Chuck grinned, unlocked the truck and handed over the keys. "C'mon, I'll go with you." The smell of stale cigarette smoke clung to the upholstery and the clutch creaked when depressed.

They drove around the neighborhood and back to the gas station.

"It seems like what I want, Chuck. Now the big question. How much are you asking? I'm ready to pay cash."

"Cash sounds good to me. I won't haggle with you. Supper's on and the wife is waiting. If you've got nine hundred bucks she's yours." Chuck leaned against the fender and lit a cigarette.

"Tell you what, Chuck. I'll give you eight hundred. You gas her up and I'll take care of the registration. Deal?"

"What the hell, make it eight-fifty and she's yours. I know you won't be sorry." He patted the fender with his hand like he would a dog.

David grinned once more, shook hands with Chuck and pulled out his wallet. He waited while Chuck backed the truck over to the pumps and filled it with gas. Then Chuck withdrew the registration from the glove compartment, signed it and dropped the keys in David's hand. They shook hands again and Chuck left. After David was out of sight, he circled the block and parked the truck a block in front of where he left Sheila. He didn't want anyone to see the truck and the car near each other. After he told Sheila about his purchase he said, "Follow me at a distance. We'll find a supermarket with a large parking lot and leave the car. It should be a few days, hopefully, before they find it."

They continued north on Route 99 throughout the night, stopping only for snacks and to buy clothes at a convenience store more in tune with their truck. David bought a cap with "Raiders" on the front, jeans, and a sweatshirt reading "Farmers Feed America." Sheila found a plain cap and through its back loop she pulled her hair into a ponytail. She also bought jeans and a pullover sweater. "By cracky," she said, "All we need is a load of chickens in the back."

With shared laughter, they both seemed to relax as they rode through the night.

CHAPTER SIXTEEN

They arrived in the Bay Area at night driving over Altamont Pass into the Livermore area on 580, turning north onto 680.

"We're going to stay on this side of the Bay," David said. "The raptor observatory is in Marin County, on the other side, but I think we'll be safer in the East Bay."

They followed 680 to the Highway 4 exit and then proceeded west to the Martinez exit off 4.

"There are several small motels in Martinez. I'm sure we'll find a place where the truck won't be out of place. Tomorrow morning, we can get in the commuter rush and head across the Bay to Marin."

Sheila said nothing. The excitement and fear deemed to have given way to exhaustion. She seemed glad when they found a motel and could finally rest. As they fell into bed, David put his arm around Sheila and pulled her close to him.

Fort Cronkite lies at the northern end of the Golden Gate Bridge extending west along the north shore of San Francisco Bay toward the Pacific Ocean. From the heights overlooking the coast, when the fog isn't churning in from the northwest, San Francisco can be seen in the distance. Ft. Cronkite, no longer a primary military installation, is now home to various private and quasi-public institutions supporting organizations involved in environmental research, marine mammal rescue operations, among others, and the Golden Gate Raptor Observatory. This organization, sponsored by the Golden Gate National Parks Association, is located in a World War II building in the western quadrant of the fort. Organized around 1986, through the use of skilled volunteers and a small professional staff, they track and record extensive data involving the annual fall migration of raptors along the California coast.

David steered the truck into the right-hand lane as they cleared a tunnel and approached the last exit before the Golden Gate Bridge. The massive north tower of the bridge came into view above the hills as they turned off Route 101.

"This is a beautiful place," David said. "After World War Two, there was pressure to develop the Marin Headlands. Happily it didn't happen and the entire coast northward through Pt. Reyes is preserved. We'll drive up there one of these days. I'd like you to see it."

Sheila smiled at him.

"We'll be driving through a tunnel under the hills which, I believe, was carved out of rock during the Spanish American war to provide access to the gun emplacements in the heights overlooking the Bay. The narrow, one lane tunnel is controlled by lights regulating the traffic direction."

David pulled the truck up behind several vehicles waiting at the tunnel entrance for the light to change to green. They drove through the tunnel and followed the road several miles to a lagoon where the road ended across from the pebble beach where waves swept ashore and children collected fragments of jade and other semi-precious stones. A cluster of WWII buildings was on the right and, after parking in the area across from the beach they located the GGRO in Building #1064. At the top of the steps they found the door open and stepped into a large room on the right with a conference table in the middle and bookshelves along the walls. No one was there. In one corner was a work area with feathered models of mechanical birds in various stages of construction. On the walls, pictures of birds were affixed, as well as articles from publications, and notices. Since a stairway led to the second level, David and Sheila climbed the stairs to an office area.

"May I help you?" A young woman smiled at them from her desk.

"Yes, I hope," David said. "We're looking for a relative, Sheila's aunt, Dr. Ruth Goldman." He turned indicating Sheila. "A few years ago, we believe she was a volunteer here and we're hoping you could help us locate her."

"I've only been here one year," the woman answered. "Maybe our director, Mr. Clark, can help you." She called out, "Allan," in the direction of an inner office where a man worked at his desk. "Some people here have questions. Maybe you can help them."

"Hi." He grinned as he came out to greet them and introduce himself. "I'm Allan Clark. What can I do for you?"

David extended his hand and explained their search.

Allan Clark, dressed in jeans and a flannel shirt, was in his early forties with a thick shock of black hair. He beckoned them into his office where they sat in straight chairs in front of his desk.

"If I can help you, I will. What is your aunt's full name?"

"Ruth Goldman," Sheila answered.

"That name doesn't sound familiar." He tilted his head upward in thought.

"Can you tell me anything more about her? When was she a volunteer, a bander or watcher, do you know?"

"Honestly, I'm not sure. I think she was here maybe four or five years ago. She'd be in her sixties, about five-five, thin. She's also very smart."

Allan Clark laughed, "Most of our people are very smart. I can't recall off the top of my head, but let me check our list of volunteers. We have over 300 so I might have missed her."

He opened a notebook and checked the names.

"Sorry," he said, "No Ruth Goldman. Now she might have been here some time ago and left the program. I wouldn't have any data on volunteers who are no longer associated with us."

"Well, thanks anyway, Mr. Clark. We appreciate your help. It's possible that Aunt Ruth may be using another name. Could you tell us what your volunteers do?"

As if deciding how to describe the volunteers' duties, he hesitated for a moment. "They do a variety of things. Primarily, though, we have hawk watch teams on Hawk Hill every day during the migration season. These are groups of maybe eight to ten people who identify the birds circling the heights before crossing the open water toward the south shore. Some nineteen species of raptors have been identified here. There are fourteen teams so each team reports on one day every other week. We also have smaller teams that capture and band birds so we can recover data on their migratory habits."

"Thank you," David said, "We really appreciate your help. Is Hawk Hill open to the public?"

"Yes, it is. Visitors are welcome. I'll show you how to get there. I hope you find your aunt."

Sheila and David walked down a path toward the lagoon and sat on a bench facing the ocean. Flocks of pelicans flew in low from the west, circled and landed in the lagoon. Cormorants perched on exposed pilings, stretching their wings to dry them in the warm breeze.

David and Sheila didn't say anything for a few moments as they watched the activity over the water.

"What do we do now?" Sheila said. "Obviously she doesn't use her real name."

"Do you like hawks?" he said.

"I love hawks. Always have."

"Good, let's go and count some."

CHAPTER SEVENTEEN

Every fall hawks arrive at Hawk Hill, the Golden Gate Raptor Observatory viewing point overlooking the entrance to San Francisco Bay. They arrive by the thousands, Bald Eagles, Golden Eagles, Osprey, Red-Tailed Hawks, Coopers and Swainsons, Kestrels, Merlins — altogether about twenty species migrate from the north and mid-west, down the California coast to points south. When they arrive at that massive break in the coastline they pause, over the north shore hills, circling, waiting for the sun and wind and the advantageous confluence of thermal up-drafts to assist their flight over the open waters of the Bay. It is here, on that wind-swept and often fog-bound hill that they are identified, counted and banded by the volunteers of the GGRO.

As Sheila and David drove over the Richmond/San Rafael Bridge, the sky was clear and sun bright. However, they could spot the traces of fog clutching the hills south of Mt. Tamalpais, on the north side of the Bay.

"What do you think our chances of finding her are?" she said.

"Your guess is as good as mine. It's our only lead."

They exited off 101 and instead of turning right to drive through the old military tunnel, they went left and then right ascending the road that rose up into the hills paralleling the coastline.

They reached the crest where the road becomes one lane and winds downhill toward the ocean where the trail to the summit of Hawk Hill begins. After parking the car, they proceeded toward the trail entrance. As they started climbing, the sun broke through the fog swirls below them over the waters of San Francisco

Bay. A cool breeze swept through the trees from the ocean to the west.

Sheila shivered. "I should have brought a sweater."

At the summit they passed a concrete platform that once supported one of the guns protecting the Bay. Across the summit, they saw people with binoculars, searching the sky. As they drew near, a tall, thin man, wearing a wide-brimmed hat with tufts of silver hair protruding, approached them.

"Hi," he said. "Welcome to Hawk Hill. We're busy counting and recording hawks. If you have any questions please feel free to ask."

The people stood in pairs in four quadrants, surveying the sky around the summit. As a hawk was spotted they would report the sighting to a person sitting on a cement platform in the center. "Adult Red-tail. Heading into south quadrant."

The birds usually couldn't be seen without binoculars and often the watchers used a spotting scope to verify identification. David and Sheila watched the process and sometimes were able to see a bird as it circled close to the summit. The view of San Francisco Bay and the City of San Francisco was spectacular as the fog continued to lift. Below them the great red towers of the Golden Gate Bridge rose in majesty over the silvery waters of the Bay.

"Is she here?" David whispered.

"No."

"You're sure?"

"I'm sure."

"Well," he sighed, "Let's leave."

They wandered down the trail to the parked truck where David leaned back in the driver's seat and rolled down the window letting a taste of salt enter with the sea breeze.

"It looks like we'll be coming back here for the next thirteen days," he said.

Sheila leaned over, put her arms around his neck and kissed him. "I'll remember to bring a sweater next time."

"Male harrier." The woman kept her binoculars focused down toward the valley below as she called out the sighting. The bird was gliding low over the field against the hills rising across the valley. "He's heading into your zone, north. Been counted."

"It's her. It's Aunt Ruth."

"You're sure?"

"Positive."

Each morning for the past five days they had climbed up the trail to the top of Hawk Hill and every day they left the hill, discouraged but committed to return. They never said it to each other, but they both knew that was their only hope of finding Aunt Ruth.

Sheila strolled over to where the woman was focused on following the course of the harrier. Her partner was a man seated on a rock nearby scanning the horizon. For a moment Sheila stood next to the woman before speaking in a low voice.

"Excuse me. Mind if I ask you a question?"

The woman continued scanning through her binoculars. "Not at all. What can I tell you?"

"I was curious. How could you identify that bird as a harrier?"

"If you see a raptor gliding low over the ground it's probably a harrier. That's their habit. But the giveaway is the white mass of feathers just above the tail."

"Oh, I see." Sheila paused. "Have you been doing this very long?"

The woman continued sweeping the horizon. "For a while."

"I think maybe I've seen you here, or someplace before. Do you recognize me?"

The woman didn't answer.

Sheila bent down and whispered in her ear. "Aunt Ruth, it's Sheila. Look at me."

"What do you want?" she whispered, as she continued scanning the horizon.

Sheila placed her fingers around the woman's wrist. "Please, Aunt Ruth, Look at me. It's Sheila. I just want to talk to you about my father."

The woman pulled her wrist free and continued peering through the binoculars. Sheila sat next to her in patient silence until she put the binoculars down. Without any expression she studied Sheila's face before speaking.

"Just follow me and don't say anything."

Ruth walked over to the man recording the sightings and said that she was taking a break. He nodded, and Ruth and Sheila began walking down the trail. David trailed behind until they stopped at a bench, somewhat removed from the hawkers at a point overlooking the entrance to the Bay below them. Ruth sat down, gestured Sheila to join her, and then said, "Who's that man you're with?"

Sheila took a breath. "That man is, how can I explain him? He's the brother of the woman my father married after he left us. He is a friend, our friend, Aunt Ruth. Trust me."

"Trust you?"

Ruth looked around. Then seeming to be satisfied, she began to laugh. "This is very funny, very funny." She laughed again, and said, speaking more to herself than to Sheila, "She finds me. Everyone else from the Gestapo to the FBI can't and she does. It's really very funny. Okay, Sheila, what's his name, anyway?"

"David, and he's a friend."

"Okay, get him. I'll go lie to my day leader, and we'll find somewhere to talk. This is so funny I can't believe it."

After they picked their way down the trail to the road where the cars were parked, Ruth said, "We'll go in your car."

"We only have a pick-up truck. Just room for two. By the way, I'm David Green."

"We'll squeeze in. Only going down the road to a look-out point where there are benches."

David realized she didn't want them to see her car so he nodded and they managed to get in and drive to the lookout. It was late morning and there were no other people at that particular spot. They parked and selected a bench overlooking the Bay, Aunt Ruth in the middle.

"Why are you here?" she said.

"It's a long story. I don't know how to begin, Aunt Ruth. I wanted to find my father. David wanted..." She looked at him. He nodded his assent. "David wanted to find the man who, well, was married to his sister. We believe he was my father. The rest is a long story."

"Well, Sheila, and David, I suppose at this point it wouldn't do me any good to say I haven't a clue what you're talking about. I've got time. I guess I don't have a choice, so tell it all, every detail, especially why and how you found me."

David spoke. "Dr. Goldman, you don't know who I am or why you should trust me. I understand, believe me. So let me start. Maybe when I'm through it will make some sense."

Dr. Goldman nodded so David began narrating the sequence of events beginning with the phone call from Tom Osborne. When he mentioned Lee's name he paused, swallowed hard so that the tears in his eyes wouldn't show. Dr. Goldman listened, never questioning him. When he'd finished he asked Sheila if she had anything to add. She nodded, no.

Dr. Goldman didn't speak for a while. Then she cleared her throat. "And you tracked me down by that mug I gave you? That's a good one. And what makes it better is those morons have missed it completely. You both make me very happy. Okay, so now what? Where do we go from here? What is it you want from me?"

"Aunt Ruth, I can't lie to you. The only good thing that's come out of this is that David and I, well, we found each other. But I've lost a father, David a sister, and we want to know two things. First, what the hell is this all about and second, where is my father? At one point I think we would have settled for just finding my dad, but that would only have raised the inevitable questions anyway. So, I, we want to know why. If I must have every law enforcement officer in the entire country on my butt, I think I deserve some answers."

"And you think that I have them?"

"I know you have them." Sheila smiled for the first time.

"Okay. You're right. This will take time. I'm tired and hungry. Drive me back to Hawk Hill. I'll get my car and then follow me."

She led them into Sausalito where they parked in the public parking lot in the center of town, then followed her to a small restaurant facing the water where she was obviously known.

"Hi, Doc." The bartender greeted her with a smile. With an air of frequency and familiarity, she waved at him and let him lead them to a booth in the rear that overlooked the straits between Sausalito and the Tiburon peninsula. Sausalito, a lovely little community situated on the east side of the range of hills fronting the Pacific, is sheltered from the storms and warmed by the sun while the hills just west are often shrouded in fog and whipped by the ocean wind. From their table, they could see Alcatraz Island and the San Francisco skyline to the south. The sailboats and ferries glided by, forming a colorful panorama.

"What'll it be folks? Any drinks?" The bartender laid the menus before them. After they ordered iced tea, an uncomfortable silence fell among them until Ruth spoke.

"You said you want to find your father. I can't help you with that. You also want to know, as you put it, what this is all about. I'm not certain that 'knowing what this is all about' is really any of your business. I'm not trying to put you off. Its just that." She hesitated. "I just don't know how much of all this you need or want to know."

Sheila started to speak, but David placed his hand on her arm.

"Dr. Goldman," he said, "Let's just take this one step at a time. Everything is happening very fast for all of us. Let's have lunch."

With his smile, the tension in Dr. Goldman' face seemed to fade and she tendered a half smile.

"Try the crab-cakes," she said. "Specialty of the house."

Later they strolled along the waterfront. Dr. Goldman beckoned them toward a bench facing the Bay. A slight cool breeze swept in from the water but the sun was warm. A cormorant stood on an exposed piling drying its extended wings. Sea gulls flew in sweeps across the shore seeking food. Seated between them, Dr. Goldman said, "Probably the worst thing that could have happened to the three of us is this, you finding me here. You can't just return to your old lives now and deny finding me. Well, on second thought, maybe you could. I couldn't. I'm not a good enough liar for that and I don't think either of you are. So, we're sort of stuck together. It's going to take some time to figure out how to handle this. Here's what I suggest. First we clear you out of the motel. Where was that, you said, Martinez?"

Sheila nodded.

"Okay." Dr. Goldman sighed. "Follow my car to my home. You'll leave your truck there and we'll drive to Martinez and then come back. That's enough for now."

Ruth's was a Victorian style house, set high against the hills facing the Bay. In the classic San Francisco tradition, the wood frame was painted white with black shutters and a wide front porch. They drove up the circular drive leading to the front, parked, and Dr. Goldman ascended the steps to unlock the front door, while Sheila and David unloaded their belongings. As they stood with their suitcases at their feet in the foyer, Dr. Goldman said, "I assume one bedroom is what you want." Without waiting for an answer she led them up a flight of stairs to the second floor and a spare room. "If you want to be alone and freshen up I'll be downstairs."

When the door shut, David put his arms around Sheila and they stood in the center of the room, hugging each other for a while. Then David tilted her chin upward and lightly kissed her on the lips. "Things could be worse," he said.

"Assuming that no one followed you, you'll be safe here." Dr. Goldman motioned them toward the sofa opposite her in the living room, when they joined her downstairs. "I can tell you a great deal, but I'm at a loss to know how it will help you."

"First, Aunt Ruth, I just want you to know how happy I am to have found you. My mother would have liked that. Why don't you just fill us in and then we'll see where to go from there. This is truly a beautiful home. I love the way you have it decorated. How long have you lived here?"

In her sixties, Ruth Goldman was a short, slender woman with delicate hands. Her fingers seemed quite long, with nails cut back, unpolished. Her thin face featured high cheekbones and a small mouth framed by thin lips. Her intense, pale blue eyes and graying hair, tied back in a bun, completed her facial description. She relaxed in her chair, folded her hands, and appeared resigned to this intrusion into her life.

"I've lived here ten years. This house was the home of my dear friend, Caroline. We met on Hawk Hill, became close friends and eventually she invited me to live here. Caroline was an old spinster, like me, never married. She died two years ago and I just stayed on. As far as I knew, she had no family, no close relatives at all, so I've paid the taxes and bills and kept the place. We were very close. I miss her." Her voice broke and she paused.

"Now I won't wait for you to ask. I know you want to hear about your father. It's extremely complicated, but I'll try to simplify things, if that's possible. I don't know. I met your father at the Jefferson Institute in Washington. I have my doctorate in biology and the institute was working under NIH grants on the human genome and related studies on factors influencing differentiation. That is how these cells become one type of cell or another. The human genome project was in process, but they were focusing on nuclear DNA whereas our focus was on mitochondrial DNA. Your father and I proposed the project that received the grant. I enjoyed working with him. He was, is a brilliant scientist and we became unusually close friends. Now things get a little complicated and difficult to tell. Just go along with me. We seemed to discover, or perhaps observe is a better term, a pattern of interrupted differentiation in certain cell lines. We were able to induce discrete differentiation. After cells differentiate they develop extracellular matrix. Cells would, after differentiation, apparently continue to normally function in every respect except in aging. We applied batteries of tests and found these cells were impervious to interactions that normally speed aging. The aging characteristic seemed suspended. This suggested enormous potential interventions in disease therapy, but we were unable to initiate or decipher the process. It was randomly observable."

Ruth stopped and stood up. "How about some tea?" Both Sheila and David nodded so she left the room returning, in a few minutes, with three cups and a sugar bowl, placing them on the table in front of the sofa. She then brought in a china teapot. As she poured the tea, neither Sheila nor David spoke, realizing Dr. Goldman would continue when she was ready.

"Well, then, everything went crazy. It was my fault. We had ongoing experiments with certain stem cell lines. The results were all orderly, programmed, disciplined. But one of these programs deviated. Deviated, I suppose, is as appropriate a term as any. I was the one to discover it. I was single, as you know. Everyone had families to go home to, but often I would stay late at the lab. I told myself it was because of my deep involvement in the work, and that's true I want you to know. I was deeply involved. But, I must admit now, it was also because of the loneliness of going home to an empty apartment. I wasn't one for the evening bars. So one night I was there, alone, and saw this deviation. In all past experiments we had no clue to the process, as I said. But this time I noticed an observable intermediary special substance in the extracellular matrix. In a certain subject, some cells secreted a protein that appeared silvery under the microscope. I was able to purify the protein. I applied a minute amount to several other cells and over a period of time I was able to conclude that the liquid material was the causative agent in interrupting the aging or growth process. I was able to generate a supply of the protein by using a specific antibody to extract the substance, and I accumulated a substantial amount. Then I made my great mistake. I reported my findings to Tom."

As Sheila and David absorbed Ruth's information, she took a drink from her cup, rose and walked to the window overlooking the Bay. "Sometimes I sit here in the evening watching how the setting sun illuminates the city. This is so different from where I grew up. I try to remember things back then, in my youth, about the city and our home, but those are dim, opaque images. California, however, here in the Bay Area, is beautiful and the people are so free and friendly. I truly love it." She returned to her chair and set her cup down.

"My companions saw things I didn't imagine. They were right and your father, Sheila, understood and had the knowledge, the vision of the potential that I lacked. Think of it. Just think of it for a moment, what it would mean if we had the ability to arrest the growth of normal cells without interfering with function. We could arrest the disease process. That's what I believed. They saw something more. If we could arrest aging in single or even cluster cells, how about the entire organism?

A small, select group of scientists led by your father, Sheila, elected to explore those possibilities. I was included only because I discovered the process in the first place. I won't go into all the details. It isn't necessary, for it's painful. Suffice it to say, the process apparently worked. Remember, these were human cells that generated the substance so the experiments were on humans, the scientists themselves. That was all the way, off course, obviously beyond all bounds, and kept very secret. But these people, me included, sensed something. How can you describe it…freedom? If this process could function on an entire organism, we would stop aging."

Sheila stood up, her mouth open. "Stop aging? How can someone stop aging? I don't understand."

Ruth leaned forward and stared at Sheila. "I told you this would be difficult, but you wanted to know, didn't you? Do you want the rest, about your father?"

Sheila nodded.

"They injected themselves," Ruth said. "This was all done without any pre-planning or experimentation. Frankly, I don't know what experiments they could have done and managed to keep secret at the same time. Time was the measure. It worked. They apparently stopped aging. There was a catch, however. It seemed necessary to continue with periodic injections to maintain the condition, and my serum reserve was dwindling. We decided it was necessary to obtain funds to research the serum creative process, in other words to discover the basis and replicate the original cell mistake. That's when they brought in the outsiders, the officials. Everything became highly organized, well funded, and supported with great promise."

David interrupted. "Let me get this straight. What exactly are you telling us? That this stuff, this fluid, serum you call it, can stop aging? In humans? For how long exactly?"

Ruth studied David, a slight trace of smile at the corners of her mouth.

"Frankly we didn't know. The aging process ceased. The organism continued to function normally."

"This is getting heavy," David said. "If I understand you, you discovered a substance that indefinitely stops humans from aging. Is that correct?"

"Let me qualify that a bit," Ruth answered. "It was much too premature to draw absolute conclusions. The process apparently stopped aging. We didn't know for how long it would be interrupted or what the long-range effects might be. Everyone involved seemed to have only one thing in mind. They all wanted it."

"This is unbelievable," Sheila interjected. "But what happened to my father and to my mother?"

"And my sister, while we're at it," David said.

"I knew it would come to this." Ruth said. "This will be painful. I won't mince words. Your father, Sheila is brilliant, as I said. I had the highest respect for him and, as you know, I loved your mother. We were very close. Your father was engrossed in the process. He experimented on himself and it worked, or it apparently worked. He wanted to include your mother and you. I believe he truly wanted to give you a gift. Your mother wouldn't go along. I believe she feared more for you than herself, but she refused to take part."

"Do you know why she refused? She wasn't a scientist."

"Yes. Sheila, I do know." Ruth said. "She refused because I told her to."

The first lights could be seen in the city across the Bay. The waves glistened golden in the light of the setting sun.

"I think that's about all I can handle at this time," Ruth decided. "Let me show you my garden and then I'd like to hear about each of you. I've been doing all the talking and now it's your turn."

David sat on the edge of the four-poster bed and surveyed the room. Against the opposite wall were a mahogany French armoire and a matching chest of drawers. Above the chest hung a framed watercolor of the Golden Gate Bridge at sunset, while to the right of the chest was a half-length mirror framed in matching mahogany. Sheila was unpacking her suitcase and arranging her clothes in one of the drawers.

"I didn't pack for an extended stay," she said. "How long do you think we'll be here?"

"Hard to say. There're still many things that we have to clear up with your Aunt Ruth. By the way, I like her. At least, for now, we're safe and comfortable. Things could be much worse. I'm too tired to think about anything more tonight. Let's go to sleep."

Sheila unbuttoned her blouse and tossed it on a chair next to the chest. She turned to the mirror and put her fingers to her face. David had switched off the main light and entered the bed so only the night light on the stand illuminated the room. Sheila traced the contours of her right cheekbone and cheek with her index finger while facing the mirror.

CHAPTER EIGHTEEN

Whn Sheila and David arrived downstairs the next morning, Ruth greeted them with a smile and a dining room table prepared for breakfast.

"Coffee is ready. That's how I start the day, strong and black. There's orange juice and English muffins. What else would you like? Cold cereal? Or I can make eggs if you wish."

Crossing to Ruth, Sheila hugged her. "I just want you to know how grateful we are for taking us in and helping us. The coffee, juice, and muffins will be just fine for me."

"I'll second all of that," David said as they pulled chairs away from the table and sat down.

The sun was rising in the east and its light streamed through the bay window when they cleared the breakfast dishes and re-entered the living room.

"Okay, so you found me." Ruth began the conversation. "Now what do you plan on doing?"

"I've been thinking about that, Dr. Goldman," David said.

"Please David, considering everything, the name is Ruth. Okay?"

David smiled. "Ruth it is. I'm beginning to get some ideas, but we desperately need more information. We don't want to interfere with your routine, and I hope we're not too much trouble for you."

For several seconds only silence dominated. Then Ruth said, "My routine, right. Just what do you suppose my routine might be? I go to Hawk Hill with my group for one day every other week. Sometimes I'll go there on other days to visit, but not regularly. Since Caroline died it's been lonely. I know those people are looking for me so I'm careful about where I go, but the truth is, I'm not motivated to go to many places. Days can be long. I watch the clock to see if it's time to eat, or shower, go to the library, or listen to the news. Activities become rituals to make time pass. I have no one. So the truth is, you two, how can I say it, properly? Perhaps I'll just leave it that I'm glad you're here."

David felt embarrassed. "Well, Ruth, we're grateful." After a pause he introduced a change in the subject. "Yesterday you told us how this project at the Jefferson Institute changed. Obviously something happened that caused you to leave and have the whole government searching for you."

Ruth sat back in her chair, gazed out the window over the Bay, and spoke as if recollecting her own thoughts rather than addressing David.

"They created a powerful, clandestine organization. It's a study in psychology to see how the promise of eternal youth can motivate people. With precious little research and fewer results, they were able to enlist anyone they approached, straight up the government hierarchy. Money was no object. Everything was kept very secret and special facilities were created around the country so that no one place could be readily identified with the project. People were regularly relocated, also, so that only a select few had knowledge of the overall program. I was one of those. They actually didn't want me, but they operated on the supposition that I was key to solving the replication process."

"Tell me about my sister," David said.

The chair creaked as Ruth left to stand near the window, her back to David. "That's the most painful part," she admitted. "When I met you yesterday, I realized that sooner, rather than later, you would ask about your sister. Sheila, this will also answer questions about your father. David, before I begin, I just want you to know how terribly sorry I am about your sister. I didn't know Lee very well. I wish I had and maybe things might have been different. Tom Osborne left Sheila and her mother when he believed, rightly or wrongly, that they would age and he wouldn't. He felt it better for them that it be that way. I think in that respect, at least, he was trying to be honest. Then he met Lee and they married. I don't know how much about the project he told her. Probably not much at the beginning. They moved regularly, as you know, and I didn't become close to Lee."

David walked over to her. "Why did she kill herself?"

Ruth turned from the window and faced David. "She wanted to please her husband so she took the serum. She wanted to have children and she became pregnant. As I told you, no one knew much about the stuff…what consequences could arise. The result was that the serum affected the normal, healthy embryo. It wouldn't grow, mature."

"My, God," Sheila exclaimed. "That's horrible. That poor woman. What did they do?" She joined the other two at the window.

"She aborted the fetus." Ruth continued. "Then Tom came up with another idea. They would develop another fetus through in vitro methodology. He believed that this might avoid the problem so they went ahead with this, but it didn't work. A fetus was implanted in Lee with the same result as the first. However, this time she refused to abort. The rest you know."

David headed for the door and stood on the porch leaving Sheila and Ruth to see the morning sun lighting the city across the silver streaked waters.

Several minutes later, David came back in and addressed Ruth. "There's still one piece of this I don't get. Where did you fit in to all this? Why are you hiding from them?"

"There are some things that are difficult to explain, for me that is. I don't know how much Sheila told you about my past but I guess I've seen enough of the dark side of this life to be bitter and cynical. I hope I'm not. I was helped by the most wonderful people anyone could wish for but I grew up without a family…no parents, brothers or sisters, or even aunts, uncles or cousins to relate to. Perhaps this had some morbid effect on me." She gave a half smile. "The truth is that I didn't care about extending my life. There are times, many times that I remember, when I thought about ending my life. Now, don't misunderstand me. This wasn't some sick fantasy. I just thought that I didn't have much to live for and if I got old and sickly there wasn't anyone who could look after me, or care. There wasn't that much more for me to accomplish in my life. Doctors would probably call this a state of pervasive depression. I suppose they would be right. That was just the way things were and are. So here I was, in the midst of these crazed people, driven by some outrageous dream of immortality, and I could care less, that is, until it all happened with Lee."

"You said you didn't know her that well." David prompted her to continue.

"That's true. But when that happened, with the babies, before she killed herself, I visited with her and we spoke. I felt so sorry for her and blamed myself, believe me, for my indifference to the whole business. You see, I prided myself on my aloofness, the idea that I was superior to those driven, sanctimonious idiots. This self-imposed dissociation vanished when I saw Lee. I felt guilty for missing the human consequences of the whole mess."

"And then? What happened?"

"It's simple." Her tone was low and matter-of–fact. "I left."

"You just left?"

"Well, not quite. I destroyed the serum, the mother cells, and all copies of my notes."

They decided the truck was too dangerous to leave in sight and since it was out of place in front of the hillside home, they parked it in Ruth's garage, one large enough to store the truck and her car. They drove into Sausalito where they bought groceries and personal items. Ruth then drove them again to the heights overlooking the approaches to San Francisco Bay where they stopped and occupied one of the benches overlooking Golden Gate Bridge below them.

"What do we do?" It was Sheila who asked the obvious question.

"You know you can stay with me as long as you like." Ruth said.

"That's kind of you, Aunt Ruth, but we can't stay here forever. David, your thoughts?"

"You're right. We can't just hang out forever. I have some thoughts, I need a little more time and information. Ruth, you said you destroyed all your notes when you left Jefferson. Is that completely accurate?"

"Well, David, let's put it this way. You can't destroy what's in the memory. I'm a scientist. Does that answer your question?"

He smiled at her. "Not completely, but we'll let it go at that for now." As he spoke he realized how fast he'd come to feel at ease with Ruth, and sensed that she reciprocated the feeling.

"Jefferson Institute was a federally funded institution, isn't that right?" he said.

"Yes, actually it was qualified as a special organization, an FFRI, Federally Funded Research Institution, by congressional enactment. I never really understood what that meant."

"But they operated under specific grants and contracts, is that correct?"

"Yes," she answered.

"Now tell me, you wouldn't, just by chance, happen to have copies of the contracts under which the project was conducted?"

Ruth stood up, placed both hands on David's shoulders and gazed straight into his eyes.

"Do you really think I would walk off with research contracts, that I would think of doing such a thing?"

He detected a twinkle. "Well, I could only hope so. And, just one more thing. I'm pushing my luck, I know, but the hierarchy, you know, the high levels in the government, do you have names?"

"David darling, I just made your day. I have it all." She tousled his hair and chucked him under the chin. "Dr. Osborne told me everything."

Sheila burst into laughter.

David spent the next two days reviewing Ruth's notes and the Jefferson contracts. He questioned her at length about the organization, the research activities and the specific names of every person involved. With patience she answered each question and explained the technical aspects in terms he could comprehend. He was a quick learner and spent a considerable amount of time on her computer. During those periods, Ruth and Sheila talked or sat in the garden or on the porch. David didn't take time to explain any thoughts or plans he had, and they didn't press him, but on the third night he announced that he would prepare his favorite meal, roast leg of lamb. As they gathered around the dinner table, Sheila lit candles while Ruth uncorked a bottle of merlot.

David raised his glass, "To the three of us. No matter what happens I'm glad this has brought us together." They clinked their glasses.

After dinner, David lit a fire in the fireplace and they finished their wine in the living room. Aware that they were waiting for him, he began. "I have an idea, a plan on what we can do."

They nodded.

"This is dangerous, I realize, but we can't go on like this indefinitely. We can't just run away. I owe it to my sister. I owe it to both of you. So this is what I have in mind. First, understand, I want the two of you to stay right here. I'll be leaving for a while. Just believe in me, and we'll put an end to this nightmare. So, this is what I have in mind."

CHAPTER NINETEEN

Sheila stopped Ruth's car where David indicated. Then she looked at him and tried to smile. "David, I'm frightened. I hope you know what you're doing." She reached over and put her arms around him, pressing her cheek next to his.

"I'll be all right. Don't worry." He kissed her, opened the door, and stepped outside.

"Now turn around. Back onto 80 north and over the bridge. Stay there until you hear from me. Everything will be fine." Without a backward glance he walked away toward his office building three blocks to the right.

The day was one of those Bay Area October days, with a clear sky and warm sun. He straightened his tie, clasped his briefcase and entered the building, where the security guard acknowledged him with a smile and a wave as he pressed the elevator button. He glanced around but saw nothing out of the ordinary. The elevator arrived and, as he'd done for years, he entered it and exited on the third floor.

Marina looked up from her desk. "My God, David." She ran and hugged him. "I've been so scared. Those people have been all over the office and I had no idea what happened to you. Are you all right? What are you doing here? Is it safe for you?"

"Everything will be fine, Marina." He disentangled her arms from him. "Come on into my office." They sat in armchairs in front of his desk facing each other.

"I can't explain everything, now. There isn't much time." He raised his fingers to his lips and motioned around the room. She nodded.

"I've been involved in some things regarding Lee's death. I think I've most of it resolved and soon things will be back to normal. But what's happening here?"

He unzipped the briefcase and withdrew a jewel case containing a CD and handed it to her.

"Nothing very special," she answered as she tucked the CD into papers on his desk. "I have all your calls listed for you, but there's nothing serious. I returned the important calls and everything can wait until you're ready to get to them. Your mail is also stacked on the desk. Again, nothing urgent. I deposited the checks that came in and paid the bills. The only call that sounded somewhat urgent was from Corey Tenet. That was right after you left. He hasn't called back."

"Good," he said. "I'll go over my mail, return some calls and then I have some errands to run."

He squeezed her hand, smiled, got up, walked around to his desk and sat in his swivel chair. Marina picked up the papers with the CD and took them to her desk as David scanned his mail in a cursory manner, selected some pleadings from a current case and stored them in the briefcase together with a pen, some of his calling cards and a yellow legal pad. He left his office and, as he passed Marina, said, "Don't worry,"

I seem to be telling everyone not to worry and that's exactly what they'll do.

He shut the door behind him and took a deep breath.

As he started across the parking lot he glanced skyward, feeling the warm sun on his face. A slight breeze ruffled his hair. He smiled at a stellar jay scolding him from a tree limb.

He felt good to be alive on such a day.

They didn't utter a word. One grabbed his right arm, the other his left and ushered him rapidly toward the black car that stopped in front of them. They frisked him and directed him into the back seat. He didn't know what to say or if he should say anything. He knew, of course, who they were and what they were doing, so he showed little surprise. The men positioned themselves on either side of him in the back of the car as the driver drove off. He noticed the man to his right pulled his pants up a little as he sat down so as to maintain the crease. Each wore a dark suit and white shirt.

"I'll take the briefcase, please." Without waiting for a reply, the man on his left took the briefcase from David's hand. After he opened it, inspected inside, felt the pockets with his hand, he closed it and set it on the floor between his well-polished black shoes. The man on David's right produced a piece of white cloth.

"I'm going to blindfold you," he said. "But I won't cuff you unless you force me to."

David nodded and said nothing. The ride continued with David in darkness, his hands folded in front of him on his lap. He tried to concentrate, think about the plan he made, how he had anticipated this, but he couldn't. He listened for sounds that could be recognized. Were they on the Bay Bridge? Was the sound of the wheels on the pavement different? Could he gauge the time they were traveling? He realized how much his ability to comprehend such information depended on his sight. He was truly sensory blind. He sat back against the car seat and concentrated on relaxing his shoulder muscles. Beads of sweat curled down through the blindfold.

When the car stopped, the doors opened and the men left, but David remained alone until he was guided out. Two men led him into a building, talking only when they gave directions, "Step up," or "Step down." Although he could hear voices, he couldn't distinguish what was being said. He was escorted down a corridor and into a room where they directed him into a chair. When they removed the blindfold, the sudden glare blinded him and he shut his eyes for a moment. He squinted as his eyes adjusted to the light. He recognized John King standing in front of him and shuddered. Next he saw agent Fallon who sat behind a table writing on a pad. Two men in military uniforms stood near the door. The men who had brought him here were gone.

"Mr. Green," John King spoke. "You will do exactly as you're told. No questions. Is that understood?"

David nodded.

King motioned to one of the men in uniform, "Take him now."

The men grabbed each of his arms and with force escorted him out of the room, which wasn't what he had anticipated. He expected to be questioned at length and at once. Instead, he was taken down a series of halls with plain doors spaced on either side, until the men halted before one of the doors and a guard produced a ring of keys, selected one and turned the door lock. The room, about ten by twelve, had plain white walls, no windows and a fluorescent light fixture recessed in the ceiling, covered with a metal grill that also covered an air vent. In one corner was a cot with a mattress on it. In another corner was a toilet without a seat and next to it a metal sink on which sat one clear, plastic cup. Over the door, a camera mounted on a metal stand focused its eye inward. The two guards stood near the entrance as David entered the room.

"Take off your clothes and place them on the cot," one of the guards ordered. David folded his pants and coat and put them down. He removed his shirt, tie, and set them on the pants and coat. Then sitting on the cot, he removed shoes and socks.

"Everything," the guard said in a rote, expressionless tone. David removed his watch, then his shorts and undershirt and put them with the other clothes.

"Now stand near the toilet." He moved to that location, feeling self-conscious in his nakedness. The second guard then gathered up the clothes and returned to stand by his companion at the door.

"You'll be given three meals a day. They'll be delivered on a tray through the slot at the bottom of the door. When you're finished eating you'll return the tray through the slot with everything on it. I mean everything that you haven't eaten, plastic utensils, cups, plates, and leftovers. Is that clear? If you don't return everything, you won't receive another meal." Without waiting for an answer he and the second guard, who held the clothes, left the room. In the ensuing silence, David heard the door being locked from the outside.

He stood still, near the sink and glanced around the room, noticing all the things that were missing. First, of course, were clothes.

I'm destined to remain naked.

The cot, welded to rings set in the floor, had a mattress with a gray cover, but no blanket or pillow. There was a roll of brown toilet paper on the floor next to the toilet. The sink contained the plastic cup, but no soap and, there were no towels.

I'll miss brushing my teeth.

David lay on the cot and, by instinct reached for a cover, a sheet or blanket before realizing there wasn't one. He cradled his arm behind his head and shut his eyes.

These assholes aren't going to break me.

He fell into a deep, dreamless sleep.

He awoke and stared at the ceiling. The only sound he heard was his breathing and the hushed tone from the air vent in the ceiling. He glanced at his wrist before realizing his watch was gone. Time had no meaning here, anyway. The light from the fixture radiated throughout the room with warm air from the vent. The few shadows were indistinct and gray. Sitting up, he placed his feet on the floor, a mosaic of gray tile receded to a water drain in the middle of the room. When he stood up, he felt self-conscious as he regarded the camera over the door. Then he began walking around the room next to the walls, familiarizing himself with the minutia of detail. His mobility was limited to walking perhaps four or five steps in any one direction, standing still, or sitting or lying on the cot.

This environment was static, a constant of white light, white walls, silence, and even temperature. No day, night, winter, summer.

He sat down on the edge of the cot and put his head in his hands.

I didn't anticipate this. How long will this last? It can't be too long. How do I cope with this? Survive?

He lifted his head and licked his lips. "Hello," he said and was surprised at the sound of his voice. It emphasized how quiet the room was.

"Hello, everyone. What's for dinner tonight?" He laughed at his words resounding in his ears.

They're listening of course and laughing. No more feeding them.

He walked to the sink, turned on the faucet, filled the cup and drank from it, then let the water run until he realized that it didn't warm up. He returned to the cot and wondered when the meal would come.

The tray slid under the door. He picked it up and returned to the cot where he set it down. The tray held a plastic plate with what appeared to be meatloaf, gravy, whipped potatoes, green beans, a slice of white bread, a butter packet, carton of milk. A paper napkin wrapped around a plastic glass, spoon, knife, and fork.

Why was the spoon there?

After he finished the meal, he slipped the tray through the slot under the door. He could see the edge of the tray and watched to see when it was removed.

They'll come and get me soon. They're treating me like this to soften me up, scare me. But they'll come soon because I have the information they want. I know that. Just remember that, keep control, don't panic.

But they didn't come. He found it hard to sleep for any length of time in the light and would awake sweating and imagining sounds in the constancy of silence. At first David was self-conscious in his nakedness, going to the toilet knowing the camera was watching him. He was aware that his beard was growing and that he couldn't shave or brush his hair. When he'd wash his hands and face at the sink, in the cold water, he'd rub himself on the mattress to dry off. He counted the number of meals served and kept track by making small scratches on the wall near the cot. This way, he believed, he could calculate the number of days he was there.

Each time a tray was pushed under the door he half hoped, expected the door would open and a guard would enter. It didn't happen. Although he had promised himself he wouldn't talk, he began mouthing words, clearing his throat, to break the silence. At last he surrendered and began carrying on discussions with himself.

Think of Lee. Think of her and of Sheila.

"Hello, Lee. Hello, Sheila. I'm all right, hear? I'm all right. I'm all right."

He would change the pitch and speed of his speech to give variety and would carry on discussions with himself, recalling books he'd read, while pacing the periphery of the room.

He realized he forgot to make the scratch for the last meal and wondered how many other meals he had also forgotten. The count was lost. Time was no longer translatable in terms of meal-days. He fell on the cot, covered his eyes with his arm and began sobbing. The soft warm air sifted throughout the room bathed in white fluorescent light that cast no shadow. Five days had passed since he entered the room.

When he heard the door unlock the sound was intrusive, the first sound other than his voice that he'd heard since being locked in the cell. He sat up and watched as two uniformed guards stepped inside and closed the door behind them. One of the guards held articles of clothing and several small packages.

"Stand near the toilet," one ordered. David obeyed.

The guard, holding the clothing neared the cot, and placed all the articles on the mattress before returning to the entrance, next to the other guard.

"On the bed is underwear, socks, slippers, and a jump suit," guard number one said. "There's also soap, a towel, toothbrush, toothpaste, razor, shaving cream, and a comb. Pick everything up and follow us. We'll take you to the shower. After you shower you'll get dressed in those clothes and leave everything else in the shower room."

After the guard opened the door and stepped into the hall he indicated that David should follow him. The second guard took up the rear. As they walked down the hall. David felt chilled by the change in temperature. The shower room had the smell of disinfectant, several showerheads spaced about ten feet apart, and metal commodes against the wall facing the showers. With no partitions, the room was lit by recessed fluorescent lights, similar to those in the cell, the only light source. He selected a bench from a row of benches near the entrance, dropped the clothes, comb and towel on the bench and proceeded to the nearest shower with the soap and shaving supplies. The guards near the door didn't take their eyes off him. The hot water from the shower felt good as he washed his hair and soaked his beard before shaving. He took his time. The guards didn't hurry him. When he finished the shower, he dressed in the clothes and combed his hair as best he could without a mirror. Stacking everything in a pile on the bench, he looked to the guards.

"Follow me," one guard said. and they exited from the shower room in the same order with David walking between the two men. They guided him into a room that appeared to be a small library for there were bookshelves along two of the walls and a rectangular table in the middle. Against one wall was a table on which sat a coffee urn, a carton of half-and-half, plastic cups, and a box of sugar packets. At the table opposite the entrance, Maureen Fallon talked on a phone. When they entered the room, she said something in the phone and hung up.

"Have a seat, Mr. Green," she indicated a chair at the table while the guards stood on either side of the closed door.

"A cup of coffee?" she said. "If so, help yourself." She nodded toward the coffee table. At the table he poured a cup of black coffee and returned to the conference table.

"You're going to be interviewed, Mr. Green. When everything is ready, I'll take you to the location where this will happen. My advice to you is to answer completely and honestly. It will be in your best interest, believe me. Don't ask any questions of me because I've nothing else to say to you."

Avoiding eye contact with David, she cradled her coffee cup a moment before drinking. They remained in silence for about twenty minutes before the phone rang. She picked up the receiver, listened for a moment, replaced it, and stood up. "Time to go." She motioned to David.

The first guard opened the door. David knew the ritual so he followed the first guard with Maureen Fallon and the second guard at the rear. They walked down the hall and approached a door where the first guard knocked. Another guard inside opened the door into a large office. On the far side, opposite the entrance was a broad, mahogany desk. One straight-back wooden chair stood in front, and to the right a flagpole bore the United States flag. Behind the desk, in a reclining leather chair sat the honorable William Devon, Justice of the United States Supreme Court.

Judge Devon nodded to Maureen Fallon, "Thank you, Agent Fallon. You and the officers are excused."

Without waiting for them to leave the room, he turned to David, "Sit down in front of the desk." The remaining guard stood near the door.

"Do you know who I am?" he said, leaning forward in his chair and staring at David.

David didn't respond.

"No, of course you wouldn't." He turned to papers on his desk and picked one up.

"Let's see, born in Berkeley, father was a stock broker, mother didn't have a college education, sang in church choir, went to U.C. Berkeley, majored in psychology. Psychology? Hmmm, wonder if you learned anything helpful. Graduated upper third. Nothing sensational. No demonstrations, speeches, arrests. Were they demonstrating in Berkeley when you were there? They're always demonstrating at Berkeley, aren't they?" He glanced up for the first time facing David who didn't speak.

"Boalt Hall Law School," he continued, glancing down again at the papers. "Average grades, middle of class. No honors. No Law Review. Passed bar the first time, well, that's an accomplishment. Clerked in San Francisco for two years, probably some nondescript law firm, civil litigation, run of the mill, wrongful discharges, landlord and tenant, contract breaches. No record of appellate work, of course. Opened your own office in Emeryville, same type of practice. Oh, look here. Here's something, two major civil suits. You actually tried and won those two cases. Nice recoveries, nice fees. You must have furnished your office then, instead of leasing furniture. You hired Marina, also. Yes, we have her file here."

Judge Devon again regarded David, wearing the orange jump suit and slippers.

"That is a sparkling record, Mr. Green. You must be very proud. You're everything a lawyer is supposed to be, right?" He paused.

David didn't respond.

"All right, Counselor Green, attorney, licensed, certified, officer of the court, I'll tell you who I am. I'm William Devon, Justice of the United States Supreme Court, a forum in which, I'm certain, you'll never appear. Consider, however, that this is your opportunity to redeem yourself, or no." He seemed to reassess his thoughts. "Perhaps I should be kinder. This is your chance to impress me, show your true spirit and ability."

His tone changed from condescending to businesslike. "Consider yourself under oath, counselor. Let's dialogue, shall we? Do you have anything to say?"

Unsure if this was truly an invitation to speak or rather another pretentious pause in the judge's monologue, David waited until he realized he was expected to respond.

"Why am I here?"

"Why are you here? Good question. You're here to make a decision. You have two options to choose from. Tell me where Dr. Ruth Goldman is and you're free, or refuse to tell me and you go back to your nice cubbyhole. I should, in all fairness, add a footnote for your consideration. I'm very busy and have neither the time nor patience to play games with you. So if you choose to remain our guest. I hope you enjoy the meals. And, yes, one other thing. If we find her without your help we may just forget where you are. Have I answered your question?"

David stroked his cheek with his right hand. His smooth cheek felt strange. He studied Judge Devon for several long seconds.

"Actually, Judge Devon, you haven't, not in the least, not at all."

Judge Devon's voice became angry. "I haven't, have I? All right, shall I tell the guard to take you back to your cell? Is that what you want?

"Go ahead, tell him. If you were serious you wouldn't have asked, now, would you, your honor?"

The judge leaned back in his chair and smiled. "You do have balls, don't you? Perhaps, maybe, I misjudged you somewhat. All right, counselor, tell me, what do you want?"

David rose and walked toward the edge of the desk. The guard at the door started to move forward, but Judge Devon waved him off. David rested his hands on the edge of the desk and leaned forward facing the judge.

"Well, for starters," he composed his thoughts with care. "I don't like being pushed around. I don't know what you and your goon, John King, are up to. I don't know why you're so damn interested in Dr. Goldman, and frankly, I don't much care. Now if you think you can intimidate me by locking me up like some animal, go screw yourself."

Judge Devon appeared to restrain his anger.

"Tell us where Goldman is, and you and your friend Sheila Osborne are free to go. I give you my word."

"Why, so you can kill her like you probably killed Tom Osborne?"

Judge Devon's eyes widened and his face flushed.

"Kill her? What do you think we are? Let me tell you something. You think you're so clever and you have it all figured out. You know nothing. You haven't a clue as to what you're talking about or involved in. You want to know about Dr. Osborne? I can arrange that also, but you better stop talking nonsense and start thinking."

David removed his hands from the desk in front of him, and returned to his chair. He spoke in measured tones.

"I have been thinking, Judge. I had time to do that, thanks to you. It's too late to just part company. You see, I've met Dr. Goldman, spent quite a bit of time with her. She's confided in Ms. Osborne and me. We know about the project. Now, what would make you think that I'd just walk away from that?"

Like a chess player who's just taken a knight, David allowed a hint of a smile to play on his lips. "Am I beginning to come through to you?"

"All right, Mr. Green. I'm starting to sense something here. Continue please. Where are you heading with this?" Judge Devon sat back in his chair. He wasn't smiling.

"I'm no fool, Judge. I don't consider myself a saint, but I wouldn't want to be part of anything that was criminal or cruel. At the same time, I guess, I'm motivated by desires that everyone has. Do you understand?"

In rapid, clipped tones the Judge barked, "Oh, yes I do. You're coming through loud and clear. Maybe I misjudged you, counselor, suffice it to say. However, I now understand. Stand up and approach the bench."

David stood and when he was once more at the edge of the desk, Devon said, "Look at me, Mr. Green. Look closely, carefully into my eyes and listen and comprehend what I'm about to say to you. Don't you ever dare judge me, do you understand? I've dedicated my life to my country, my family. I've honored the rule of law. You set yourself above me with your smug assertions about criminality and cruelty. What have you ever done that makes you think you can pass judgment on me? "

"Granted. So where does that leave us?"

Judge Devon's face softened to a smile.

"I like you, David. I'll call you David from now on. Again I think I misjudged you. I must admit I did wonder why you exposed yourself so easily at your office after eluding our agents for so long. It seemed too easy even for someone I didn't have a high regard for. Now it makes sense. Here's the deal. We need to locate Dr. Goldman because she's the only person who can show us how to continue. She has the key and we must have it."

"I know Ruth Goldman," David said. "She won't give you what you want. Just how do you propose convincing her to give it to you?"

"David, you underestimate us. I won't torture her. You know that. I don't have to. You majored in psychology, right?" He didn't wait for an answer. "What I propose is to encourage our good doctor to make the right decision. It's not nice, but it will work. We'll place her in a position where she must choose between two unacceptable alternatives. Remember Tryon's novel, Sophie's Choice? The premise of the story was that when a person must make a choice, even a horrible choice, between unacceptable contradictions, a choice will be made. Sophie had to make a choice between the lives of her two children. Pick one to live, the other to die. Make no choice, both die. Make a choice and at least one lives."

David's voice quivered. "That's ghastly. How do you propose to do that with Dr. Goldman?"

The Judge smiled. "Don't worry," he began with a tone intended to be reassuring. "We'll make it much easier for her. We'll give her a choice between an abstraction, that is the formula, and a real life."

"Whose life? I'm afraid to ask."

"Now don't get upset, David, but it will be Sheila Osborne."

David stiffened. With a mouth dried, he licked his lips. "You're really crazy." His voice was almost a whisper. "For a moment you almost had me convinced. You'd really stop at nothing, wouldn't you?"

Judge Devon pointed a finger at David and laughed. "You disappoint me. Instead of letting your testosterone control, use your mind, for God's sake. You're smart. Stop and think. This isn't a choice between two lives. Dr. Goldman really has no choice. She'll choose life. She'll give us the formula without a second thought. Oh, we'll scare her for sure, convince her that we are serious, to make it easy. Perhaps we'll let King growl at her."

He stopped and chuckled at his wit. "But even if she has doubts about our sincerity, even if her gut tells her we wouldn't do it, she'll never take the chance. We win. Hey, it's better than tossing her naked in one of our cubby-holes, right?"

"You're a real shit, aren't you?"

"If you say so. Now, are you ready to become a shit, also? Do you want in?"

"Convince me."

"Convince you?" The judge started laughing again and had to recover before he could speak. "I'm laughing at you and at myself. I ask myself why I take such crap from a nobody like you. I should be angry, but I'm not. It's funny, actually. You had me fooled at first, I admit that. Now you have yourself fooled. You want me to convince you to sell you on the idea of immortality. I must make you feel good about accepting this gift that you want with your entire being. But, I'll indulge you because I'll let you in on a secret. I believe that you can be a real asset, not just a passive beneficiary. We, you and I, can do things, counselor, accomplish great things, together. I'm offering you a contract you can't refuse."

David leaned across the desk and grasped the judge's hand. Judge Devon's face showed an impulse of anger. David withdrew his hand and said, "Okay, I accept. But…"

"There's a but to this? What is it?"

"I want a face-to-face with Tom Osborne. Just the two of us, alone."

"All right, counselor. Motion granted. I pity Osborne. Now can we get started? I'm due in Washington tomorrow."

At last David smiled.

CHAPTER TWENTY

It had been a week since Sheila dropped David off near his office.

"Stay there until you hear from me. Everything will be fine."

Those were his last words.

She and Ruth stayed close to the house, venturing out only for supplies and walks nearby, and, during those days both of them recognized their developing friendship.

"How about a picnic today?" Ruth proposed one morning. "We'll have it on the front porch near the phone and with the view of the Bay. I never will get used to that view, especially on clear evenings when the setting sun reflects off the City. Is there any other place in the world as beautiful?"

Sheila slipped her arm around Ruth's shoulder and hugged her. "I'll make turkey sandwiches and we have a bag of chips. Lunch is a bit early for cocktails, but how about a cold one?"

"You betcha," Ruth answered. "We've got'em on ice."

The fog was low that morning, sweeping in through the Gate, obscuring the bridge except for the great towers. This was living fog, unlike the still mist that haunts the redwood groves to the north. It flows with force and speed, expanding, retracting in snake-like currents. By noon it would substantially dissipate and the sun would begin to warm the atmosphere. The City would again emerge from the mists, skyscrapers first, reflecting the new sun, and gradually the remainder, like a new Brigadoon.

"Do you get into the city very often?" Sheila said.

Seated on the lounge chairs they faced the Bay. There were two mugs of cool ale on a table between them along with the remains of lunch and a bowl of chips.

"Not too often," Ruth replied. "I make a point of going to some of the performances of the symphony and opera. Sometimes I'll go in and walk along Union Street just to be part of that young upbeat crowd. I gain energy from them. In truth, it was more fun when Caroline was alive. But, I try." She smiled, reached over and patted Sheila's arm. "Perhaps you and I will go in soon, when all of this is history. We'll shop in the boutiques and drink lattes in one of the sidewalk cafes. Would you like that?"

"Yes," Sheila answered as she squeezed Ruth's hand in response. "I'd like that very much." Then she hesitated before speaking again. "Aunt Ruth, there's so much I don't know or understand. This aging process…you tell me you can stop aging. Is it a simple judgment that this is either bad or good? I understand there are deep moral principles involved. But let me ask you a simple question. Do you ever look in the mirror? You know what I mean? Do you touch your skin, notice the shadows growing deeper in the lines on your face? Do you see yourself aging and ever wonder, maybe I could stop this process? We women spend millions on creams and lotions advertised to stop or reverse aging. You might have the ultimate answer. Have you thought about that?"

Ruth smiled. "How easy it is for me to open myself to you. I'll try, be as candid and honest as I can in answering your questions. And don't worry about asking these things. We're all involved in this and we have to be open with each other." She sighed before continuing.

"I don't look in mirrors. I'm an anomaly, Sheila, a living ghost. I should have died with my family those many years ago. Every time I look at myself in the mirror I face this overwhelming depression and guilt. Who is this person staring back at me, chosen to survive, grow older, when all the others died so young? Why me? The image in the mirror is a distortion as if cast through cracks in the glass. I'm an aberration, Sheila, a fortuitous mistake. I survived for no apparent reason. So for me, what purpose would there be in extending this error?"

Before continuing, Ruth glanced away for a moment.

"I don't want to sound morose. I try to be up-beat, but it has been difficult since Caroline died. We laughed together. However, there is one thing I want to make very clear. Life has been good to me. When I think of the beautiful people who befriended me, helped me, risking their own lives, I know that I've been incredibly lucky, blessed. I'm forever grateful."

When Sheila rose to put her arms around Ruth, Ruth whispered, "Now you and David have come into my life. What more could I ask for?"

They finished the picnic, cleared the table and went into the living room where they chose the two leather reclining chairs positioned on each side of the great stone fireplace on the south wall.

"How did you come to this country, Aunt Ruth? The last I remember was your telling me about when a woman named Rose came to the orphanage for you. Who was Rose?"

"You ask who was Rose. Rose, Rose Cohen. Are you familiar with the term a woman of valor? No? Well I'll tell you where it comes from, but not now. Trust me when I say that Rose Cohen was an exceptional woman, exceptional person, beautiful, tall, graceful, kind, caring beyond belief. How she ever put up with that petulant teenager was remarkable."

Rose Cohen had been a war widow. Her husband was a marine officer who died on Tarawa. She became quite involved in Jewish philanthropic activities. When the war ended, and the remnants of European Jewry were struggling out of the camps, she and others went to Europe to save as many as possible, and bring them to the new state of Israel. Rose was working with children and that was how she came to Ruth at the orphanage. Sheila was too young to remember, of course, but it was very difficult to get Jews out of Europe and into what was then Palestine. Rose took Ruth to southern France, to a children's camp established by her organization, to wait for a boat to Palestine. Ruth felt confused, frightened, obstinate.

"Mrs. Cohen," Ruth said, "I'm not going to Palestine. I want to go back home."

"Ruth, my sweet," Rose Cohen responded. "I know how you feel. I understand, believe me, but you must try. There is no home for you back there. Your home is with your people in Palestine. They're your family."

Ruth broke into tears and screamed at her. "I don't know them. They aren't my people. The nuns loved me. Why can't I go back to them?"

Rose drew Ruth to her, held her close and murmured, "Because, my Ruthie, they aren't your people. They were brave, wonderful people who helped you so you could find your new life where you belong."

"Are you my people, Rose?" Ruth watched the tears flood Rose's eyes.

"Yes, my Ruthie. I'm your people." Rose kissed Ruth on the forehead and brushed back her hair with her hand. "I guess you're mine, now."

Ruth never forgot that moment.

Rose Cohen came from a wealthy Massachusetts family. Her father had emigrated from Poland in the 1890s and established a very successful wholesale kosher poultry business. Rose inherited that fortune. She brought her new charge and challenge, the orphan Ruth, to Boston.

"I was given every opportunity," Ruth continued her story. "Private schooling and Harvard University for both undergraduate and graduate studies. Rose never let me forget my family. My blue coat was cleaned and hung in a closet. We both opened the envelope that had been pinned inside…a fold of Dutch bills bound with a paper clip and a note, in my father's hand…addresses of relatives in Amsterdam. It sits on the desk in my room. Every summer we went to Israel to search for my brother, and any relatives. Never found any trace of them. But then, Rose died in my arms and I wondered, was this my fate? That everyone I'd come to love must die? But, as I told you before, I'm an up-beat person. I like to laugh, have good times. I have faith. So you see, my sweets…funny isn't it how we pick up terms…that's what Rose called me. I have faith and now I have you."

"And David," Sheila added. "I hope we hear from him, soon."

CHAPTER TWENTY-ONE

For two more days David remained a prisoner, but now it was different because he had a room, clothes, and he dined with the guards. Nevertheless, he knew, as a prisoner, he couldn't leave, so he didn't try. Judge Devon was not to be seen.

On the third day, after lunch, the guards ushered him back to the same room in which he had seen the judge. His brother-in-law was standing behind the desk with his back to the door.

"You know, David, Devon trusts you. I don't. Let's get that straight from the start. You want to get it off your chest, go ahead. It makes no damn difference to me."

As one guard left the room, the other shut the door and stood by it. David chose the chair in front of the desk and faced Tom Osborne's back. He didn't speak.

Tom finally turned around. "You can make any deal you want with the judge. I could care less. Okay? I'm here to say whatever the hell you want. Let's get it over. I never want to see or hear from you again. So get on with it."

David didn't answer. He settled back, looked around, took his time, surveyed the room and at last centered his gaze on Osborne. "I only want to know one thing. Why?"

Tom slapped his hand to his forehead and looked to the ceiling.

"He wants to know why. Just like that, the all-inclusive one word eternal question, why? Why what, David? Stop playing games. Let's get this nonsense over and done with,"

In a soft voice without a smile or other emotional expression, David said, "I want to know just what was so important to you that you would leave your wife and daughter, remarry and then drive your new wife to suicide. This may sound strange, but I believed you when I came to Virginia after Lee died. I believed then and I believe now that you loved her. So there is a disconnect here that I can't understand. Tell me, Tom, just what the hell was so important to you that you could do those things?"

Tom took the chair behind the desk and told the guard. "Get out."

The guard was startled. "I was ordered to stay."

"And I'm ordering you out. Now. Get out."

The guard shrugged as he closed the door behind him.

Tom glared at David.

"As I said before, I don't trust you, and I don't believe you for an instant. But you're correct about one thing. I did love them and I'm forever grieving over my loss. Now, that being said, if you think it was easy for me to stand in front of you and say it, you're wrong. What the hell else do you want or need to know?"

"Just why you want to live forever?"

Tom put his head back against his chair and laughed. "He wants to know why I want to live forever. That's a good one." His voice sobered. "Perhaps I misjudged you, believing you shared the same feelings and values as me. You must enjoy seeing funerals, watching the hearse haul away the rotting corpse. Graveyards must turn you on, all those cold, empty fields of stone memorializing forgotten names. Somehow, I don't accept that, so if given the chance wouldn't you want to live forever?"

"I don't know, Tom. I honestly can't answer that so simply."

"Well now, it's strange. You asked me a simple question. Did you expect a simple answer? The truth is, you can answer directly if you're truly honest with yourself." As if assured, Tom continued. "You're lying to yourself when you say you can't answer simply and you know it. You're aware that every day you get older until you get to a point where your skin shrivels, hangs loose from your limbs, your organs begin to fail, you can't see, you can't hear, you can't remember and all you know, all you really understand is that you live in pain and it can't get better so the best you can hope for is that you die quickly. Now, tell me, do you want that?"

Before speaking, David collected his thoughts. "Nobody wants that, Tom, but we accept death as the inevitable consequence of the gift of life. Good grief, is that me talking? I must sound like some preacher, yet it's true. Every living thing is born and ultimately dies so that new things can be born. That is nature, the way of life, orderly and inevitable. You want to change all of that. Have you considered the consequences of interfering with the natural order?"

With his voice certain, Tom let David finish before he spoke. "But we do it all the time. Every time you take a pill, have an operation, get inoculated you interfere with the natural order of things. The entire science of medicine is calculated to do just that. Doctors cure and prevent illness. That is good, isn't it? And, don't they extend life expectancy? In our time, life expectancy has been extended by around ten years. If they could extend it longer, wouldn't we applaud them?"

"You're obfuscating the issue," David said. "It's one thing to extend life expectancy. It's quite another to eliminate aging and death. Have you truly thought through the consequences? If everyone lived forever wouldn't the planet become suffocated with people in a few generations?"

Tom rose and avoided David's gaze. Seconds elapsed before he spoke. When he did, his voice was soft, almost apologetic. "I'm a scientist, not a psychologist, philosopher or theologian. Each of us has asked ourselves the same questions you ask. It just so happens, however, we do have such people associated with us and we have discussed these issues with them. I'll try to paraphrase and summarize my understanding of their beliefs.

"We are insane, all of us, collectively, you, me, every single person on the face of this earth who is aware that they are going to die. Our core nature is total ego…love. What could be more compelling then to become aware that he, him, self must end. Of all living things only man became aware of his mortality. That knowledge was unacceptable. He couldn't live with it. He couldn't deny it, ergo the knowledge had to be negated. Thus came religions, gods, and promises of eternal salvation to conquer death and obliterate the undeniable. At last, we have the means of curing the insanity that created this monstrous, anti-rational mythology. At last, we can develop our minds, our intellects free of this horrible oppression. The search for truth can now be honest, free. You ask whether there is some inconsistency between extended life. I don't use the term, immortal. We'll all die of something someday, accident or disease. But even if we were immortal, we wouldn't be depriving our children of their rights. Firstly, only a chosen few will have the benefit of our product. At the present time, as you're aware, we don't know how to procreate and have the treatment at the same time, but we'll solve that one. Now here's one for you. Suppose everyone was offered a choice, children or immortality, what do you think the majority would choose? Before you answer, think about the consequences, creeping, painful decay or protracted youth and health. How many would give up children for that promise? Would the answer be different from the twenty year old than the sixty year old? I don't know, but something to ponder."

A momentary silence prevailed as David absorbed Tom's comments.

Tom continued, "Are you a religious person, David?"

"That's an irrelevant question."

"That's the lawyer talking. No it isn't irrelevant. I'm serious. Let's put it another way. Do you believe in a God, a Creator?"

"Tom, this is going nowhere."

"You wanted answers, David, so I'm trying to accommodate you, and all you actually want is to confront me, to vent your rage. Truth is, you don't know what you believe or what you want."

"You can think what you wish, Tom. However, there are some rules to this game. First, I won't be your pawn to make a point. Second I won't be goaded by slights and barbs. So if you have something else to say, speak up."

A hint of a smile appeared and then vanished from Tom's mouth.

"The point is simply this. If we are the creatures of an intelligent creator, and, this is a big "and," the creator is caring, loving, why would He inflict us with the horror of growing old and inevitably dying? Aging means pain, shriveling organs, horrible diseases. What possible reason would such an omnipotent and caring being have for inflicting this upon the ones he created with love? Perhaps He wanted and expected us to use the intelligence He gave us to overcome these miseries, to challenge us to think, to reason. If we were born to just sit around fat, happy, disease-free, what motivation would there be to think?"

He paused, perhaps waiting for some response.

"I'll tell you what I believe, David, in all truth and honesty. I can't conceive of any mystery or challenge beyond the capability of man to comprehend. That is my belief and my religion."

Now David didn't hesitate in his response. "So why all this pontificating about God and morality and such? You're doing all this for yourself, not for some great purpose. You're not out to save civilization from suffering. This is all about you, just you, your precious life, and a few of your rich, or powerful, or very bright friends. The rest of the world be damned."

Tom laughed. "Your choice of words is eloquent, although I'm certain you didn't intend it that way. But you're right, in a narrow way. This is about a small group and there isn't any monumental philosophy underlying it. Ultimately the world will be better because of us. Suffice to say, that's enough justification for me, even if I don't need it."

"So, Tom, I'll ask you the same question you asked me, earlier. Do you believe in God, a Creator?"

"David, you're a good lawyer. I always knew that. Yes, you do deserve an answer. Truth is, my friend, I don't particularly need God at this time. However, it's time to conclude this meeting. I'm unsure if I've answered you. I respect you because we shared a love for a wonderful woman. You ask me why? My answer is, I want to be truly sane, free to develop my mind to the best of my abilities. Perhaps I will be able to give something of value back to mankind. Is that asking too much? There is one thing I'll ask of you."

He withdrew an envelope from his inner coat pocket and handed it to David.

"This is for my daughter. I want her to know that I love her and want a relationship with her. That, of course, is up to her, and you. Be good to her, David. I feel you two will be happy."

Accepting the envelope without comment, David deliberated for a second and then walked toward the door. As the knob turned in his hand he said to Tom, "I can't answer your question. Neither can I justify the price you paid for your decision. I only know that there is something wrong, deeply wrong."

CHAPTER TWENTY-TWO

"Sit down, Mr. Green."

John King indicated the empty chair on the opposite side of the table across from him and Maureen Fallon. They were in the same room he'd been interviewed in by agent Fallon prior to meeting Judge Devon.

After David sat down, King continued.

"The three of us are going to meet Dr. Goldman. We want to make this as free of complications as possible. That's why you're coming with us, Mr. Green, so that you can assure her that we mean her no harm and that we will be returning to Washington immediately and you'll be with us. The plane is at San Francisco International. Any questions so far?"

"What assurances do I have that you will free me when you have her in custody?" David said.

"I guess you'll just have to trust me. Frankly, you don't have a choice in this matter."

David leaned forward in his chair and pointed his finger at John King. "So once you have her in custody, why must I go to Washington? Explain that, please."

King stood up. "I don't have to explain anything to you. Is that clear? Now pick up that phone and call Dr. Goldman. Tell her that you want to talk to her, that it's important but you can't talk over the phone. Tell her you are on your way and she should wait for you. Now do it. By the way, Agent Fallon will be monitoring the call, so play it straight."

David shook his head in thought before he picked up the phone and dialed Dr. Goldman's home.

"This is David," he told her.

"Oh, David, I can't tell you how glad I am to hear your voice. Sheila and I were so worried. Are you all right?"

"Yes, yes, I'm fine. I need to speak to you but not over the phone. You understand. It's very important."

"Of course. I understand perfectly. When will you be here?"

"I'll be leaving in a few minutes."

"Good, we'll be waiting. We're eager to see you. Hurry, David."

"I will." After he hung up, Agent Fallon nodded to John King that all went as scripted.

"Good," King acknowledged. "Let's get with it."

Once out of the room, they continued along a hallway to an elevator that delivered them to a parking garage where a black, unmarked limousine and driver were waiting. Agent Fallon sat next to the driver while David and John King sat in the back.

"All right," King began, "What's the address?"

"I don't know the address, but I do know how to get there. It's in Sausalito. When we get to Sausalito I can direct you."

"I guess that's how it will be, then. One detail, though, Mr. Green. I'm sure you'll understand. A blindfold until we are away from this place. Then I'll remove it."

David stared at King. He couldn't keep the hint of a smile from forming at the corner of his mouth. "Sure, like I'd really want to come back here."

King secured the blindfold over his eyes and they proceeded in silence.

David could hear the sounds of the City, a cable-car bell, the thump of tires on cobblestones, and knew when they were approaching the Golden Gate Bridge. King untied the blindfold allowing David to see the sun highlighting Alcatraz, a freighter being escorted by a tug toward the port of Oakland, and sailboats darting in the wind that swept through the gate.

"Where do we go now?" King said.

"Exit Sausalito and go into the main section of town."

They proceeded down the winding streets that led from the highway to the shore, and along the beach into town, this day mild and sunny with light breezes. Tourists were out and the streets busy with traffic.

"Turn left at the next light, just past the park, then, where it forks, continue left."

The narrow streets took them into the heights above the town and the shimmering Bay below. The setting sun cast shadows from the balustrades and eaves of the buildings in patterns on the street.

"This is it."

David indicated Ruth's home set back from the street at the head of the crescent driveway. The limousine drove up the driveway and stopped in front of the house. No one could be seen as they exited the car and ascended the front steps. John King grasped the bronze lion head doorknocker and knocked twice.

From inside, Ruth's voice called, "Come in. The door's open."

King advanced into the house with David. Agent Fallon followed behind. They entered the living room where Ruth sat on the sofa facing the door. On her right was Sheila. On her left was Marina. In the chair beside the sofa sat Corey Tenet. Behind Corey stood a uniformed United States Marshall.

As the front door closed behind Agent Fallon, King turned to David. "Who are these people? What's going on here?"

Before David could answer, Corey rose. "You're John King, I presume. I've been expecting you. I'm Corey Tenet, Assistant U.S. Attorney for the Northern District of California." He produced his wallet and presented his official identity card to John King. "This young lady," nodding toward Marina, "has some documents for you."

With that, Marina stood, approached King, and handed him papers.

"Mr. King," she said, "I'm serving you with two court documents. The first is an order of the Federal Court, Ninth Circuit, restraining you, your agents, the FBI, and all federal agencies from arresting or in any way taking involuntary custody or control of Dr. Ruth Goldman. The second document is the complaint in an action initiated by Dr. Goldman, alleging a conspiracy to defraud the government and naming you, among others, as a defendant."

The documents rustled in Kings' tight grasp. Marina returned to her seat as Corey Tenet explained further. "Mr. King, by the nature of Dr. Goldman's suit, initiated under a provision of the federal False Claims Act, the Department of Justice has the right to intervene on behalf of the plaintiff and assert the government's rights to prosecute the case. That decision has been affirmatively made. You might be interested to know that service of process is being effected presently against all the other named individuals including the Attorney General, the Vice President and specifically named cabinet officers. Because this could and probably will result in the appointment of a special prosecutor and in convening a special grand jury, I suggest it is in your interest to say nothing. Incidentally, Dr. Goldman is under the protective custody of my office, so I recommend that you say good-by and clear out right now, read the documents carefully, and get yourself a good lawyer. You'll need one."

In a low voice, King whispered to David. "You did this. I knew you couldn't be trusted."

"You should have trusted your instincts. See you in court, John. I can't wait."

King skimmed through the restraining order, looked toward the U. S. Marshall and then at Agent Fallon.

Agent Fallon stared at King. "I suppose it was too good to be true."

"We'll leave," he said. Then to the others he announced, "This isn't over yet. Not by a long shot."

"You're right," Corey agreed. "This is just the beginning. It's our turn, now."

As John King and Agent Fallon left the house, the others watched from the porch as the car descended out of sight. Then Sheila ran to David and threw her arms around him.

"My God, you can't believe how worried we were. I'm so glad you're all right." Tears filled her pale violet eyes. "Let's celebrate. I'll haul out the champagne."

Ruth burst into laughter. "Just seeing the expression on that man's face when Marina gave him the papers made my day."

Corey Tenet turned to David and they hugged each other. "David," Corey said, "All I can say is you've got guts. I was going to use another term, but the marshal is present." Everyone laughed, including the marshal.

"This is a work day. Of course we aren't supposed to drink during working hours, but if the marshal won't tell, neither will I."

When Ruth reentered with the champagne and glasses, she insisted, "David, you must tell us what happened to you. Let's sit down and hear it all. I can't wait."

"Well," David began as he lifted his glass, "It's a long story."

CHAPTER TWENTY-THREE

Rachel Devon wheeled herself into the library where her father had spent most of the last two days, secluded from the world and his daughter.

"I need to talk with you." she said. "Isn't it about time we faced this thing together?"

The morning papers were spread on the table before him, his name prominent in the headlines.

"Rachel, my darling, what can I possibly say to you? I've let you down. I've let you down big."

She wheeled her chair close to him and clutched his arm.

"I'm sorry that you feel you can't trust and confide in me. After all, when everything is said and done, we only have each other."

He smiled, a weak smile from a defeated face. "I really thought I knew it all. How wrong I was. I wanted everything for you, but I realize now that I wanted it for myself, also. Rachel, my darling, I don't know what I wanted more. I must live with all this now."

"It's not over by a long shot," she said, a touch of petulance in her voice. "We'll fight this thing all the way. After all, don't we have the two best lawyers in the world on our team? I've already started researching the law. Let me see if I've got it straight. The False Claims Act dates back to Civil War days, but was recently amended to permit private whistleblowers to bring suit and recover penalties and damages. It's called Qui Tam, Latin meaning acting on behalf of the king as well as himself. Some incentive for them. They could get rich."

"Rachel, listen to me. You're beautiful, with an incredible spirit. How lucky I am. I love you, I love you more than life, and I would do anything to make you happy. Now you must trust and believe in me. Everything, and I mean everything alleged in the complaint about me is true, down to the last detail. I won't dishonor our name any further by denying it. Tomorrow, I'll submit my resignation to the court. I'll notify plaintiff's counsel that I will not interpose an answer to the complaint. Then, do you know what we'll do? You and me? I think we'll take a long vacation someplace, where we can spend all that overdue time together and perhaps discuss further aspects of the Japanese internment cases. What say you, counselor?"

Tears streamed down her cheeks as she hugged her father.

"I must abide by the court's ruling. So, how about a cruise?" she whispered. "Perhaps to the South Pacific."

On the table beside her chair by the window in the bedroom, Sheila laid the letter from her father. She hadn't read it during the excitement of the past days as she needed time to collect her thoughts and feelings, but, most of all, she needed to be alone.

I wondered if he really remembered me or cared. Now I suppose I'll find out.

She opened the envelope flap, withdrew, with care, the undated letter handwritten on plain paper, and held it to the morning light streaming through the paned glass.

My Dearest Sheila,

I'm certain this letter is as difficult for you to read as it is for me to write.

I'm not the type to express my feelings. Indeed I sometimes wondered if I really had any feelings. But after all the events of these past weeks I came to realize how much I lost when I left you and your mother. How very much I would like to become a part of your life again. I don't ask for forgiveness, perhaps just a mote of understanding. You should know that I left because that was something your mother and I agreed would be best for you. By now you know the entire story of the project and my participation. Believe me when I tell you I wanted nothing more than to have your mother and you participate with me. It was, of course, her decision not to do so. I honored that choice.

How strange it is that you have found David. What a bizarre turn of events. Who could have conceived such a thing? But I believe he is a fine, honorable man. I wish both of you nothing but happiness. I only wish there was some way for me to share that happiness with you. That, however, is up to you. At the end of this letter is a set of directions on how you can reach me if you should ever wish to do so. Nothing would make me happier. However, I'll understand if that isn't your desire. Just let me leave you with one final thought. I love you dearly and wish you the peace, joy, and happiness you deserve.

Your father

Sheila folded the letter and replaced it in the envelope on the table.

After David left for the office, Sheila and Ruth sat on the front porch sipping tea. Sheila smoothed her windblown hair with a sweep of her hand.

"Aunt Ruth," she said, "I can't believe it's over. I'm so relieved."

Ruth smiled as she crushed a lemon wedge into her tea. "I don't think it's really over. But, I suppose as far as we are concerned, it probably is. I would like to breathe fresh air again. But that brings me to another question."

She raised the cup to her lips. Ruth then said, "What about you, Sheila? What happens with you, now?"

"What happens with me?" she repeated, a little surprised at the directness of the question. "I haven't had time to think about it."

"Well, I'm sure you've thought about you and David."

Perceiving the direction of Ruth's comment, Sheila smiled. "I honestly don't know. You see, we've never discussed the future. Everything has been so hectic. We've been living from day to day. I can tell you this much. I deeply care for him. You know what I mean. I hope he feels the same way. Beyond that I don't know. I suppose I'll return to Albany. I've almost forgotten about my life back there. We'll have a lot of things to talk about and to find out where we are in our relationship."

Ruth nodded. "There's one thing I want you to know, just tuck away in the back of your mind. This is a big house, a very big house. I'm sure I could find room for a young couple here."

"That's sweet and thoughtful of you."

Ruth's smile broadened. "It's not just that I'm magnanimous. I'm very self-sufficient, as you know, but I also happen to be lonely."

"I understand, yet I'm perplexed about something else. There is one thing I can't understand or figure out."

"And that would be?"

Sheila twisted in her chair, swiping at her hair. "You said you destroyed your notes with the serum and left nothing behind. You said you had no personal interest, ever, in this process. Does that mean it's gone forever?"

Ruth stirred her tea, took another long sip of Earl Grey, and ran her tongue over her lips. A touch of a smile lifted the edge of her mouth.

"Sheila, my sweet, suffice to say only this. Never underestimate the iniquities of an old woman."

David entered his office at 8:45 a.m. and proceeded to gather the mail stacked on the reception countertop, but Marina would have no part of this business-as-usual routine and ran from behind her desk, scattering papers in the air, to throw her arms around him.

"Oh, my God, I can't tell you how happy I am that you're back. I don't know where to start or where you should start. Go in your office, sit down and I'll bring in the coffee. Business can wait. I want to hear everything. Especially about Sheila." She winked at him.

David laughed. "That's a woman for you. Here I've laid my life on the line and she wants to know about my new girlfriend."

He picked up the mail and, once in his office, leaned back in his chair, wrapped his arms behind his head and realized, how wonderful it would be to get back to a normal life.

Marina carried in two mugs of coffee and demanded, "I want to hear it all."

"Ahhh." David relished a drink of his favorite French roast before he smiled at Marina. This woman knew how to brew his coffee, run his office, and advise him on any subject, personal or business. He had trusted her with his life.

"Where to begin, Marina. Let's see, hmmmm. Well, there was this young woman with violet eyes and a coffee cup from the Golden Gate Raptors Observatory."

The phone rang and, as Marina answered it, her cheeks paled. She put her hand over the speaker.

"It's Tom Osborne."

Coffee splashed onto the desk as David placed the mug down. The last person on earth he expected to hear from was that man.

"All right, Marina, I'll talk to him." She handed over the phone and left the room, easing the door shut behind her.

"Tom, I wasn't expecting your call." His tongue felt dry.

"David, I want to congratulate you. You were splendid."

David tried sitting back in his chair, but his back muscles wouldn't relax. Stress tightened his body causing his left knee to ache. "Thank you, but I don't know what the hell you're talking about. What's your point?"

"Hey, calm down. Just listen to me. First and most important, the letter I gave you for Sheila contains a method for contacting me. It is an internet communication website, untraceable, but it works. I want her and you, since you two are an item, to be able to reach me. Someday, when all this furor is over, maybe she'll realize that I really do love her and want to be a part of her life." He paused. "Next, and I trust that you're sitting, I said I want to thank you. You came through perfectly, predictably. You got rid of all those demanding bureaucratic leeches that were destroying everything our group is trying to do. Now, that leaves just the few of us…friends, scientists, confidents, who will continue the project. Please tell my friend and colleague, Ruth Goldman, that I harbor no grudges and still intensely respect her. Further, tell her that I know precisely what happened and exactly what she discovered. Everything she did was monitored by me. I'm sorry if all this has caused her grief, but it had to be done and, as I said, I knew I could count on you. We're doing just fine. Don't worry about me. Money can buy anything in this world and we have plenty of it. Do tell my beautiful daughter that I love her. And David, one last thing. I loved Lee, too, and will never forgive myself for her death."

David broke the connection and closed his eyes.

We were running like the wind, down from the heights on the Inspiration Look trail. The sun was setting in the west and the golden light played in dancing shadows off her hair, tied back with a kerchief.

"Race you back," Lee said. "Catch me if you can." Her laughter echoed through the trees."

Marina peeked around the door as he shook his head.

"It's only the beginning," he said.

FINI

I'm alone.

My daughter is dead.

My grandchildren are dead.

My great grandchildren are dead.

I'm alone, in this quiet room, with shelves of decaying books, ancient treatises yellowed, torn and, naturally, of course, long outdated. That is me. Torn, outdated. The room is silent because there is no one to talk to. My associates? Do I even deem to call them that now? They're gone. I don't know where. We learned, painfully, that we could only function in a social setting for a limited time. The young associates would stare at us, wonder what is it with these people who don't show wrinkles or pallor? Then we would leave, find another setting where we could begin again. I look in the mirror and I see Dorian Gray. The young, beautiful, talented women smile. After all, I was young, brilliant, wealthy. How long could such relationships last? I would leave in the night, going nowhere but away. Those associates, who came with me so long ago also learned. They're sitting alone, in some quiet room pondering their sorrow.

Can I bring a cup of tea to my lips with steady hands?

But wait, we brought genius, intellectual talent and curiosity, unfettered by time, to a desperate world. Wasn't that worth the suffering? Won't someone remember me for my gifts to such a world?

I laugh in bitterness. All that self-imposed righteousness, superiority. Goodbye daughter. I will change the world.

The skin didn't wrinkle. The tissue was frozen. The hair didn't gray or eyes pale. Still, stalled, interrupted. And so were those brain cells. Where was the flexibility of thought, adaptability of cognitive reasoning? The brain didn't deteriorate, or grow. Our new, young colleagues were centuries beyond us in comprehending the systems, functions, languages of an ever-changing world. The frozen brain was an antique.

I don't know where my associates are, or if any are still alive. I don't care. I will die someday, but I don't have the courage to determine a time. I'm human.

It's time to leave again. I'll pack my books for no other reason than habit. They're useless. I appreciate the full meaning of that term. I'll walk down some new street and perhaps a woman will smile at me.

What could it be that obsessively compels people to strive for beauty by putting letters of the alphabet together like the matched pearls of a necklace to form words, words into sentences, sentences to paragraphs and passages, all coming together in a woven wonder of meaning?

What possessed a Beethoven, morose in his deafness, to pen notes into chords, chords into bars, themes into the resounding movements of his ninth symphony, arguably the greatest composition ever written?

Could it be in the words of Milton. "There should be no moaning at the bar." Or, perhaps Byron's "…mingling with the universe to feel all that could be not expressed but ne'er concealed."

What madness inspired such thoughts? Could it be the universal melancholy call?

Remember me, rejoice in my music, feel the passion of my words, exult, tremble at my Mona Lisa, my David, my art, my craft. Do these things and I will be remembered and if I'm remembered I shall be immortal.

Is this creative obsession the ultimate struggle against the finality of death? Is such beauty and feverish motivation the child of such madness?

God, the grim reaper, dark angel, He who committed us to the tomb will pluck us, as we would pick ripe cherries from a tree, and place us upon some celestial cloud where we would, with glee and gratitude proclaim our reborn sanity and, in divine exultation, flap our feathers through eternity singing His praises.

"Oh, what fools these mortals be," cried Puck. Could it be that his laughter resounded through an empty universe?

C'est La Vie

Tom Osborne

CPSIA information can be obtained
at www.ICGtesting.com
Printed in the USA
FSOW03n0256021215
13792FS